"It'll be okay. I know it will," Val whispered.

"Sure it will." Gary tried to put conviction in his words.

"You know what Dr. Harper said. This is just precautionary." Val's words sounded hollow, as though she were trying to reassure herself as well as Gary. "The odds are in my favor."

"That's right," Gary murmured. But he didn't give a damn about odds. All that mattered was that Val should be all right, that the surgery would be successful. *Dear Lord, please make her well*, he whispered to himself. *Give us a second chance!*

Series Story Editor **Mary Ann Cooper** is America's foremost soap opera expert. She writes the nationally syndicated column *Speaking of Soaps*, is a major contributor to soap opera magazines, and has appeared on numerous radio and television talk shows.

Amanda Preble is a romance writer who comes from a family of soap opera fans. She lives in New Jersey with her husband, her word processor, and her books.

From the editor's desk...

Dear Friend,

Captivating . . . exciting . . . heartwarming . . . these are but a few of the comments we've received from Soaps & Serials readers. We're delighted. Every month the fine team of writers and editors at Pioneer pool all their resources to bring you seven new spectacular books.

Based on actual scripts from KNOTS LANDING, each novel is written with you in mind. Soaps & Serials take you back to the very beginning of the show, revealing the innocent and infamous pasts of your favorite characters, recreating cherished moments from your favorite episodes. And though each book is a complete, satisfying read, our sensational cliffhanger ending is just a hint of the drama that will unfold in next month's Soaps & Serials book.

We've recently received numerous requests for previous volumes of Soaps & Serials. If you are also curious about how it all began—or if you want to complete your collection—please see the order form inserted in this book.

For Soaps & Serials,

Rosalind Noonan

Rosalind Noonan
Editor-in-Chief
Pioneer Communications Network, Inc.

KNOTS LANDING™

11

A SECOND CHANCE

From the television series created by David Jacobs

PIONEER COMMUNICATIONS NETWORK, INC.

A Second Chance

From the television series KNOTS LANDING™
created by David Jacobs. This book is based on
scripts written by J.B. Wallenstein and Carol Roper.

KNOTS LANDING™ paperback novels are
published and distributed by Pioneer
Communications Network, Inc.

ISBN: 1-55726-200-4

Printed in Canada

10 9 8 7 6 5 4 3 2 1

Mary Ann Remembers

KNOTS LANDING

The first thing they tell you in writing class is to write about what you know. On KNOTS LANDING, producer Joseph B. Wallenstein followed that suggestion when he sat down to write his first episode for the series. And he had quite a story to tell. Wallenstein's wife, Peg, faced a crisis that shook his family to its very core. A routine medical checkup had revealed a malignancy. Surgery was necessary, and radical measures would have to be taken if her condition was even worse than doctors feared.

In Book 11 of the Soaps & Serials KNOTS LANDING series, Valene Ewing encounters a similar crisis. Much of what is said and described in this story is based on the way that Joseph and Peg faced their own personal test of courage. It is a testimony to the time-honored adage, "love conquers all."

The episode written by Wallenstein originally aired February 19, 1981. It was his own special valentine to his wife. This book is another example of KNOTS LANDING's commitment to stripping away the glitzy barrier between the program and its viewer to provide believable characters in realistic settings.

Chapter One
Unwelcome Calls

The morning was cool and clear. A strong ocean breeze had blown away the last traces of smog, leaving the mountains clearly visible, their peaks still snow-covered. Outside the window, palm trees and the bed of zinnias that the ambulatory patients enjoyed swayed gently in the breeze. It was a glorious morning, a time for rejoicing. But Dr. William Harper did not feel like celebrating.

It had been a long night. Bill Harper knew that he should take comfort from the fact that he had been able to save three of the four accident victims. Instead, his thoughts centered on the one who had been beyond his help.

It was always difficult losing a patient, especially a young one with a family. Some doctors might manage to see patients as statistics; he had never been able to be that calculating. And so he suffered with his patients, sharing their joys and their sorrows.

Yes, it had been a long and difficult night. And now this!

Bill unfastened the clasp of the manila envelope and pulled out the papers once more. Perhaps he had misread the lab results. But he knew he hadn't. The report was clear; there was no doubt of the results.

Slowly Dr. Harper reached for the phone.

"Are you sure this is supposed to help?" Ginger Ward asked. She sat up and gestured at the pillows that were carefully arranged in the middle of the living-room floor. The furniture had been moved aside, leaving a large expanse of the beautiful oriental carpet exposed. The early-morning sun streamed through the window, seeming to focus on the pillows. Ginger shielded her eyes with her hand and looked up at the slender, jeans-clad woman beside her. "I can't decide if we're having a slumber party or a sorority initiation."

Val Ewing smiled at her friend. "You're the one who wanted to do Lamaze," she reminded her. "I'm just an innocent bystander."

"You're a slave driver."

"The term is 'labor coach.' Now, back

on the floor and let's practice relaxing."

Ginger placed her hand on her rounded stomach as though considering. "This baby better be worth it," she groused, but she placed the pillows beneath her head and legs.

"First is a cleansing breath," Val said, consulting her book. "You have to take a deep breath, then exhale deeply."

Ginger complied, ending on a giggle. "I can't believe I have to learn how to breathe."

"'Through the use of the principles of controlled breathing, the pregnant woman is able to control her labor and minimize the pain.'" Val's voice was schoolmarmish as she quoted from the textbook, and Ginger's giggle became a full-fledged laugh.

"I thought *I* was the teacher," she said.

"Not here. C'mon, Ginger, let's practice."

Under Val's direction, Ginger alternately tensed and relaxed each part of her body.

"You're right," she admitted a few minutes later. "I do feel better."

As Val turned the page, reading the next exercise and studying the picture so she could explain it to her friend, Ginger sat up and refastened the clip that held her strawberry-blond hair away from her face.

"Remember the day we met in Dr. Bender's office?" she asked. "You were there for a checkup, and I didn't want to believe I was pregnant. Look where it got us. Here I am, my stomach like a watermelon, and you're stuck being my coach."

Val laughed. "You know I don't mind," she said, then quickly lowered her eyes, pretending to study the Lamaze book. The day she and Ginger had met in the gynecologist's office, Val had been there for her appointment to find out why she and Gary had not been able to have a child after Lucy. When they had moved to Knots Landing, they had hoped to start a new life, a life that included a baby. But so far, it hadn't happened.

"Let's try again," she said to Ginger, and then remembered how many times she had said the same thing to Gary, but with a different meaning. Brushing those thoughts away, she turned back to the textbook. Ginger needed her, and Val was not one to fail a friend.

The Westminster chimes of the grandfather clock signaled the half hour. "I'd better go," Ginger said, slowly getting up and pulling the top of her gray sweat suit down over her rounded abdomen. "If I relax too much more, I'll never get to school. Although," she added with a chuckle, "I could use a little relaxation. Those kids keep me busy every minute." She took the book from Val and hugged it closely in an oddly protective gesture. "Would you mind if we practice at night from now on? I keep worrying about being late for school."

"Fine with me."

As the door swung shut behind Ginger, Val smiled sadly. Lucky Ginger!

"They have *how* many kids?" Laura Avery demanded. She looked around the beautifully furnished office as she listened to the person on the other end of the line. There were times when she still couldn't believe she was actually a realtor, even more times when she couldn't believe how successful she was at it. "And they want to spend *how* much?" she asked. As she put the phone down, Laura shook her golden head and laughed. "They must think I'm a miracle worker."

"You mean you aren't?"

Laura looked up, startled. She hadn't heard Scooter approach. "Not this week," she admitted. "This couple has six children, and the house has to have seven bedrooms, a playroom, a den, a sunken living room . . ." Her voice trailed off.

"So? Beverly Hills will be perfect."

"But they don't want to spend Beverly Hills prices." She quoted the figure she'd been given, and her boss smiled.

"Now I see why you're laughing." Scooter draped an arm around her shoulders. "Why don't you come into my office? I'm sure if we look hard enough, we can find something for them." He nodded in the direction of his plush corner office.

As he smiled again, the tiny lines at the corners of his eyes deepened. It was only when he smiled that people realized Scooter Warren's true age. At other times he seemed far younger, and people were invariably surprised when he mentioned that he would soon be a grandfather. But when he smiled it was easy to believe that he was nearing fifty.

"I wouldn't want my star salesperson to lose a sale," Scooter said as he and Laura walked toward his office.

The woman whose desk was next to Laura's looked up. Exchanging a significant glance with the receptionist, she said, "There they go again."

Karen Fairgate tipped her dark head to one side as she watched Valene fold laundry. The two women were in the Ewings' kitchen, trying to talk over the gurgle and whoosh of the washing machine. "I saw Ginger leaving your house this morning. What was she doing over so early?"

As the washer began to drain, shooting a spray of water into the laundry tub, Karen offered up a silent thank-you for the fact that her house had a separate laundry room. Val's house was cute, and she'd done a wonderful job of decorating it on a shoestring budget, but there was no doubt that it was small.

"I'm Ginger's labor coach," Val explained, searching for the mate to one of Gary's navy blue socks. "She's going to take Lamaze classes, so we started the beginning exercises."

"Cleansing breaths?" Karen asked, helping herself to a cup of coffee from the pot Val kept on her stove all morning.

Val nodded. "And relaxing each part of the body."

"You'll go on to the four levels of breathing and then work on focusing. Has Ginger picked out the picture she's going to focus on?"

Val looked up from the laundry in surprise. "When did you become such an expert on Lamaze?"

"Sid and I used the Lamaze method when our children were born. I don't think I'll ever forget the night they taught effleurage."

"Effleur-what?"

Karen laughed. "They called it light abdominal massage, but it looks like rubbing your stomach. All of us women were intent on it—we took it so seriously. Then Sid caught another guy's eye, and the two of them started laughing. They cracked up the whole class."

"I had trouble stopping Ginger from laughing, and all we did was practice breathing," Val admitted.

"It's all worth it, though," Karen assured her. "It was a wonderful experience." She smiled, remembering how Sid's coaching had convinced her she didn't need anesthesia, and took a sip of coffee. "I feel so sorry for Ginger, having this baby alone."

"I know." Val put another load of clothes in the washer and glanced at Karen, her blue eyes sad. "Ginger's excited about the baby—who wouldn't be?—but I know she's worried about raising it alone."

Karen gazed at Val sympathetically. When she and Gary had first moved to the cul-de-sac, some of the neighbors had thought her a country hick, a new Beverly hillbilly. But Karen knew that underneath Val's lovely but unsophisticated exterior, behind her gentle manners and her soft voice with its faintly southern accent, was a strong young woman who had faced tragedy and refused to let it defeat her. She was a woman who cared deeply, and right now that caring was focused on Ginger.

"Sid has seen Kenny," Karen told Val, "and he says he wants to come back, but Ginger won't let him."

"Do you blame her? Every time she's counted on him, he's failed her." Val measured soap, then turned to Karen. "I think she loves him, but she doesn't trust him."

"Do you think—" Karen's words were interrupted by the shrill ringing of the telephone. "Want me to get it?" she offered.

Val shook her head and reached for the receiver.

"Yes, this is Mrs. Ewing." She listened for a moment, and Karen saw the color drain from her face. "But he's at work." Val closed her eyes, trying to control her breathing. "Okay . . . we'll be there at ten."

Val hung up the phone, then stared at it as though it were a foreign object she had never seen before.

"Val?" Karen's voice was filled with concern. "What's wrong?"

But Val did not reply. Slowly, she picked up the phone again and dialed a number. "This is Val. May I speak to Gary?" she asked, her voice oddly flat. "I see. Well, please tell him I need to see him. I'll be there in half an hour."

She replaced the receiver, then stared sightlessly out the window, her face unnaturally pale yet calm.

"Val?" Karen rose and moved swiftly to Val's side. Gently she placed an arm around her friend's shoulders and led her to a chair. "What's wrong?" she asked.

Val shook her golden head as though the motion would clear away her confusion. "I don't know," she murmured, half to herself. "He sounded so strange. Not the way he usually does."

Karen poured another cup of coffee and placed it in front of Val. "Drink this," she insisted.

Val gulped the hot liquid, and as it warmed her mouth she seemed to return to reality.

"What's wrong?" Karen asked again.

"I don't know. Maybe nothing." Val gripped the coffee cup with both hands. "I went to see Dr. Bender; you know how worried Gary and I were that I couldn't get pregnant." She picked up the cup and sipped slowly, trying to delay. Maybe if she didn't say the words out loud, everything would be all right. But Karen nodded, encouraging her to continue. "Dr. Bender found something . . . a growth . . . and she sent me to see Dr. Harper."

Once again Val's voice stopped, and she stared into her coffee cup. Then she raised her eyes to Karen's and said quickly, "He took it out. Nothing to it. Real simple." Her matter-of-fact tone defied Karen to offer sympathy, to say that anything was wrong. But then, just as suddenly, Val's composure crumbled. "Oh, Karen," she sobbed. "He wants to see Gary and me."

Karen laid a hand on her friend's shoulder. Brusquely, Val pushed it aside, pulling herself together.

"It's probably nothing. We don't know why he wants to see us," she said.

Karen nodded.

"Could be lots of reasons."

Again Karen nodded, but her eyes were serious. As Val left to meet her husband, Karen Fairgate rested her head in her hands in a timeless gesture of worry.

This was the time of day Gary and Sid

liked best, the hour before the dealership opened. They usually spent the time reviewing inventory, trying to decide which cars to push that day, planning promotions or, when there was no especially pressing business, looking at Sid's new engine. For although selling new cars was the primary business of Knots Landing Motors, his experimental engine was Sid Fairgate's first love.

Today the two men were in the back of the lot, gazing at three cars with broken windows.

"I don't suppose it was an accident?" Sid said, knowing the answer before he asked the question.

"Not unless bricks have suddenly started growing on those trees." Gary Ewing looked up at the tall palms that flanked the lot. "Last time I checked, those weren't brick trees." His words were light, but his expression was sober as he surveyed the damage. The force of the flying glass had cut the leather upholstery. The windows could be replaced quickly; the upholstery was another story.

"Damned hoodlums! I'm going to call the police." Sid turned and stalked back to the office, leaving Gary alone on the lot.

Gary gazed at the shattered window. This was the third time this month they had been the victims of vandalism. Was there a reason, or was it simply teenagers with too much time on their hands?

"Big brother said we had problems," said a seductive voice.

Gary looked up as Abby approached him, and despite himself he smiled. It was hard not to smile when Abby was around. She had hair the color of the California sunshine, and her huge violet eyes sparkled with warmth. Today she was dressed in a clingy lavender jumpsuit, which emphasized her perfect figure and made her eyes appear an even deeper shade of purple.

"I'm supposed to take an inventory," she said, indicating her steno pad and pencil. "You tell me what's damaged; I'll write it down."

As Gary turned toward the cars that had been vandalized, Abby placed her hand lightly on his arm. "This lot is so rough," she said in a voice so low that Gary had to move closer to hear her. "I'm always afraid of twisting an ankle."

The light scent of her perfume wafted through the air, and Gary found it hard to concentrate on the broken windows. It wasn't fair that a woman should be so beautiful!

When Abby had taken careful notes of the damage, she and Gary walked back to the office. "Will you help me fill out the insurance forms?" she asked.

Gary nodded. Sid had been good enough to give him a job when he had needed it; the least he could do in return was help Sid's sister with the paperwork. Besides, he owed Abby a lot. If it hadn't been for her, who knew how that disaster with Roy Lance and Frank Korshak would have turned out?

"I'll come into your office," Abby offered. She brought in the claims forms and spread them in front of Gary, then moved behind the desk and perched on the arm of his chair as he began to read them. "I never know what to put here," she said, pointing one shapely finger at a line on the form. Her head was so close to Gary's that he could feel her silken hair swaying as she leaned forward.

"It's easy," he said. But before he could continue, the intercom buzzed. Gary turned on the speakerphone. "Yes, Marsha?"

"Your wife is here. She says it's important—something about a doctor."

Gary pushed his chair back, scarcely aware that Abby was still leaning on the arm, and grabbed his jacket. He was half-way to the door when Abby said, plaintively, "We weren't finished."

Gary turned, surprise evident in his eyes. "My wife needs me," he said, and continued out the door.

A frown marred Abby Cunningham's beautiful face as she watched him walk away.

Chapter Two
Painful Words

"What are you doing here?" Ginger's green eyes flashed with anger as she caught sight of the man just leaving her house.

"I needed my address book," he answered defensively.

"Well, now you've got it, so get out." Ginger could feel the adrenaline beginning to flow. So much for the hour of relaxation exercises she had done at Val's.

"C'mon, Ginger . . ." His voice became cajoling, a tone she knew all too well. But this time she was immune. The charm wouldn't work.

"You don't live here anymore, so from now on if you need something, call." Ginger enunciated each word carefully, a technique she had learned for controlling the quick temper that she had inherited along with her reddish-blond hair. What she wanted to do was scream like a maniac. But the former Miss Knots Landing didn't scream. That wouldn't solve anything. And if she remained calm, Kenny wouldn't have the satisfaction of knowing how much his surprise visits bothered her.

She climbed the front steps and walked to the door, forcing Kenny to move aside. It was a small victory, but now she was inside the house and Kenny was the outsider.

"Look, Ginger, we've got to talk." The morning breeze ruffled his blond hair.

"About what?" she demanded.

"I won't give up," he said defiantly. "That's my child you're carrying."

"I know." Ginger put a protective hand on her stomach, as though trying to prevent the unborn child from suffering from its parents' argument. "It may be your child, but I'm the one who's pregnant." Her expression was serious as she added, "I can't trust you, Kenny, so I'm going to handle it myself."

With a sad smile, she closed the door in her husband's face.

"Why didn't you tell me there was a problem?" Gary gripped the steering wheel, driving automatically without really seeing his surroundings, and glanced over at his wife. In her simple turquoise dress with her hair falling to her shoulders in golden curls, she looked like the teenager he had married. No one would think they'd been married seventeen years, especially not now as Val sat with her hands clasped around her knees.

Valene turned her head away and gazed out the window, unwilling to face her husband. "There wasn't a problem. The doctor found something; he took it out. That's all there was to it." She watched the sprinklers along the side of the freeway, as though concentrating on them would make her problems disappear.

"It's probably nothing." Gary tried to make his voice reassuring, but it sounded false, even to him.

"Probably," she agreed.

They lapsed into a silence that lasted until they were seated in the doctor's office. Then Val reached over and grasped Gary's hand, needing the reassurance of his grip. They had been through so much together. They'd make it through this, too, she told herself fiercely.

Dr. Harper entered the room. "Hello, Val." The doctor smiled, but Val noticed that his smile seemed forced and his weary eyes were serious. He shook hands with Gary, then sat down behind his desk and opened a file folder.

For a moment there was silence as Bill Harper studied the couple in front of him. They were young, blond and more attractive than any two people had a right to be. To a stranger, they would look like a golden couple with hardly a care in the world. And he was the one who was going to shatter that illusion.

"I asked you both to be here because I like to have a couple together in these cases."

Val's face turned ashen. She had sensed from Dr. Harper's voice when he called that something was wrong; now his words and his solemn tone confirmed her fear.

"What is it?" The words seemed to escape from her throat.

Dr. Harper looked at Val, his dark eyes filled with compassion. Then he turned to Gary. "When Val was here the last time, I removed a small growth from her colon. I have the lab report in front of me."

He looked down at the paper, and Val felt her heart stop for one long moment as she waited for the doctor to speak.

"We've checked and rechecked." Dr. Harper leaned forward in his chair, as though by being closer he could soften the impact of his words. "It was malignant—cancerous."

His statement was met with utter silence. Val swallowed several times and tried to speak, but no words would come out. She turned to her husband. His eyes were closed, his face ashen.

Oh, God! Not this! Not Val! What did she do to deserve this? Gary's thoughts were a whirling maelstrom.

"Cancer?" He must have heard it wrong.

Dr. Harper nodded. "The pathology report confirms it."

Gary shuddered. What was he going to do? Val was sick, dangerously so. And she'd need his help. The question was, would he be able to help her? He and Val had been through things that would have destroyed other people, other marriages, but they had survived because Val had been strong. This time, though, it was Gary who would have to provide the strength.

Cancer! The word reverberated in his mind like a refrain, a sound he wanted to blot out but could not. Cancer! It was the loudest word Gary Ewing had ever heard.

A restless energy filled Kenny Ward. He couldn't have explained what it was that propelled him; all he knew was that he found himself parking his car at Santa Monica Place and walking the short block to the ocean. Perhaps it was nostalgia for his days as a beach bum; perhaps it was a longing for the peace the ocean always brought him. Whatever the reason, he was there.

He walked rapidly and mindlessly, his feet moving mechanically. But after a block or two his pace slowed, and he once again became aware of his surroundings.

The park was long and narrow, a tiny strip of grass and flowers between the street and the ocean. A row of trees and bushes screened the view of the cars rushing by on the highway below. Instead, the visitor's eye was drawn out to the beach and the pounding surf.

For a long moment, Kenny stood riveted by the sight of the ocean. Then the eager voices of children brought him back to the present. He turned, leaning on the iron railing, and watched a harried schoolteacher shepherd her class.

"Stay in line," she said, frustration evident in her voice. "No, Eric, don't touch the flowers."

Chuckling, Kenny walked slowly along the path. Then he stopped abruptly, his attention focused on a couple. The woman was tall, attractive and very pregnant, dressed in shorts and a top that emphasized her swollen stomach. Her companion was a bearded young man, clad in cutoff jeans and a rugby shirt.

They walked hand in hand, stopping to sniff the blossoms on one of the bushes. Unaware that he was staring, Kenny watched as the man put his hands on the woman's shoulders and bent his head slightly to kiss her forehead. A feeling of longing swept through him.

The couple began to walk again. Then the woman stopped short and reached for the man's hand. Placing it on her belly, she smiled tenderly as he gasped, his face reflecting both surprise and delight.

With a groan, Kenny turned away.

"I've got to talk to you."

Ginger stopped abruptly in the school's entrance. "Didn't we just go through this this morning in another doorway?" she asked with more than a touch of asperity. She grasped her briefcase tighter and began to move down the wide steps toward the street.

Kenny followed, then put a hand on her arm to restrain her. "I went to the park on my lunch hour today."

"Am I supposed to get excited or something?" Without waiting for him to reply, Ginger said, "*Wonderful*, Kenny!"

He flinched at the sarcasm, but this was too important for him to stop now. He spoke quickly, not giving Ginger a chance to interrupt. "I saw a young couple. She was pregnant. I guess she felt the baby kick, because she took the guy's hand and put it on her stomach." Kenny's gray eyes searched hers. "They were in it together, you know?"

Ginger stared at her husband. He sounded so sincere, as though he really cared, as though he truly wanted them to be a couple again. She wanted to believe him. Oh, how she wanted to believe him! But . . .

"I'm not sure we'd be in it together," she said slowly.

"What do you mean?"

Ginger looked down at the pavement, absentmindedly noticing that the children had drawn a hopscotch diagram on the sidewalk. "I'm sorry. I really am." She raised her eyes to meet his. "I just can't count on you."

"Sure you can." Kenny was confident.

"I wish I could, because I'd like to share all this with you." She touched her stomach. "But I can't." She brushed off Kenny's hand and walked toward her car. "Please, let's not fight. Let me do it my way."

As the car pulled away, Kenny kicked viciously at a pebble. *What am I going to do now?* he demanded of himself.

The whir of the can opener stopped, and the tantalizing aroma of coffee filled the Fairgates' kitchen.

"I wonder if she really feels that optimistic, or is she just being brave?" Karen mused.

Sid poured a scoop of coffee into the pot, then turned to his wife. She and Diana were loading the dinner plates into the dishwasher.

"Both, I guess. From what you said, there's a good chance the doctor got everything the first time."

Karen nodded. "The doctor told Val the surgery was precautionary. He's going to remove a small section of tissue above and below where the growth was to be sure it didn't spread."

As the coffeepot began to perk, Sid pulled out one of the cane-backed chairs. "I think Val is being reasonable."

Diana scraped the remains of her potato into the garbage disposal, keeping her back to her parents.

"Why do you say Val's being reasonable?" Karen asked.

"Say she assumes the worst. After the surgery, if it *does* turn out to be the worst, her pain won't be any less because she anticipated it."

Still with her back to them, Diana asked, "What is the worst?"

Karen and Sid looked at each other. In their worry over Val's surgery, they had spoken openly, almost forgetting their daughter's presence. How much should they explain? How much was a teenager ready to hear?

It was Karen who answered. "The worst is if the cancer has spread."

"But," Sid continued, "the doctor doesn't think that has happened."

Diana turned around, her dark eyes serious. "Then she'll be okay?"

"We hope so."

Diana turned back to the dishwasher, uncomfortable as she asked the next question. "There's something else, isn't there?"

Again Karen and Sid looked at each other, communicating wordlessly as they had done so many times during their marriage. They'd said this much; they owed Diana a full explanation.

"It's called a colostomy," Karen answered slowly. When Diana did not reply, she asked, "Do you know what that is, Diana?"

The girl shrugged but did not face her mother. "I think so." A moment later, she dropped the handful of silverware in the sink, turned abruptly and left the room.

Karen looked at the doorway, then back at Sid. "I'm always telling myself these days that she's a young woman, that I have to treat her like an adult. Sometimes I forget there's still a little girl inside."

That night neither Karen nor Sid could sleep. They lay in bed, silent, each pretending to be asleep. Finally Karen spoke. "If it were me, Sid? If I were having the operation . . . how would you feel?"

"I'd hate it."

Karen didn't move. "I know," she said. "And that's what Diana realizes. A thing like that could end a pretty solid love between two people."

Sid reached out and switched on the light. When his eyes had adjusted, he turned to his wife. "I said I'd hate *it*." He emphasized the last word. "It wouldn't change my feelings toward you."

For a moment Karen was silent, considering what he had said. It sounded right, but maybe it was just semantics. Then she asked, "How can you separate the two things?"

Sid sat up, propping the pillow behind him. When he looked at Karen, tenderness was shining from his brown eyes. "It's not that hard. I'd hate anything that hurt you, Karen, but why should I hate you for being hurt?"

He put his arm around his wife's shoulders and drew her to him so that her head rested on his chest, and continued, "You may be attracted to a pretty face or a nice pair of legs, but you fall in love with the person."

The tension that had filled her all day began to ebb, and Karen snuggled closer, basking in the warmth of her husband's love. "I hope Gary sees it that way," she said.

"Gary's stronger than you think."

"I hope you're right, Sid. I really do." But as she reached across him to turn out the light, a worried frown crossed Karen's face.

"Hi, coach! Sorry I'm late," Ginger called, opening the front door of the Ewings' house. But it was not Val but Gary who came down the stairs, carrying a small suitcase. Ginger looked it at questioningly. Val hadn't mentioned that Gary was going away; was this a last-minute business trip? But before Gary could explain, Val came downstairs.

For a moment she gazed at Ginger bleakly, as though trying to remember why her friend was in her living room. Then, spying the book Ginger held, she remembered. Lamaze.

"Oh, Ginger, I'm sorry." Val's voice was distracted. "I forgot. I should have called."

Ginger looked from Gary to Val to the suitcase, trying to solve the puzzle of what was going on in the Ewing household. For something was obviously wrong.

There was an uncomfortable silence before Val spoke. "I'm going into the hospital." Her tone was calm, as though she were discussing someone else, someone she hardly knew.

"For what?" Their Lamaze practice had been only that morning, and Val hadn't said a word about a hospital then. But now all the sparkle was gone from her eyes. Something was very, very wrong.

In that oddly dull voice, Val continued, "It's exploratory surgery. Remember the day we were in Dr. Bender's office? Well, she referred me to a surgeon." Val looked down and smoothed an imaginary wrinkle from her skirt. "He removed a malignant growth, and now he needs to be sure it hasn't spread."

Cancer! The word shrieked in Ginger's head. Instinctively, she put her hands on her stomach, as if protecting the life that grew inside her.

"Oh, Val!"

Ginger's distress seemed to rouse Val.

She moved forward and embraced her friend, patting her shoulder in a gesture of comfort.

"I feel awful!" Ginger stared at Val, trying to comprehend the seriousness of the situation. "I don't know what to say."

"Don't say anything. I understand."

But as Ginger walked home, her mind reeled. It wasn't fair! She and Val had gone to the same doctor on the same day, but, oh, the results had been so different! Dr. Bender had given Ginger wonderful news: she was going to have a child. Val had not been so fortunate. She was not having the baby she so longed for; even worse, her own life was in danger.

Life just wasn't fair.

"It'll be okay. I know it will," Val repeated. For the second time that day, she and Gary were in the car heading for the hospital.

"I know." Gary tried to put conviction into his words.

"You know what Dr. Harper said. This is just precautionary." Even to herself Val's words sounded hollow, as though she were trying to reassure herself as well as Gary. "And don't forget that I have everything in my favor. I'm young, female and slender. The odds are very good." She had said the words so often that afternoon that they had become mechanical.

"That's right." But Gary didn't give a

damn about odds. What were they worth? All that mattered was that Val should be all right, that the surgery was successful, and that they didn't have to perform a . . . Even in his mind, he couldn't pronounce the word. He recoiled. Val, his beautiful Val. Dr. Harper had explained that if the growth was too low in the colon, if he couldn't reconnect the two pieces, he'd have to perform radical surgery. He had gone on to explain the procedure briefly, but Gary had stopped listening. His mind had refused to consider the possibility. Val would be all right. She had to be.

The ride to the hospital that morning had seemed endless. Now it was over all too soon. Slowly they walked toward the hospital entrance, each lost in his thoughts and fears, neither able to speak. As they approached the door, their footsteps slowed still more as though by delaying they could avoid the inevitable. And still they did not speak.

Just before they reached the final ramp, Gary stopped. Wordlessly, he set Val's suitcase on the ground and drew her into his arms. With a muffled cry, she threw her arms around him, not sure whether she was giving or receiving comfort, not sure whose tears were staining her face.

Chapter Three
Comforting Arms

The smell of frying bacon filled the Averys' kitchen. Laura had read all the articles warning that bacon contained nitrates, nitrites, whatever, but that didn't stop her from serving it for breakfast. Breakfast, in Laura Avery's world, was scrambled eggs, toast and meat. She'd had to make a few adjustments in Knots Landing. At Richard's insistence, she served English muffins instead of toast, and since the markets didn't carry the scrapple that had been part of her childhood in Philadelphia, she had substituted bacon. But the breakfast she served her husband and her son, Jason, was a *real* breakfast, not the California version consisting of yogurt and fruit.

As she turned the slices of bacon, the phone rang. Laura reached across the counter and lifted the receiver. She smiled and greeted the caller with a cheerful hello, then listened for a few seconds, her smile rapidly fading. "No . . . I didn't know." The person on the other end spoke again, then Laura said, "Of course I'll go with you. Want me to drive?"

When Laura hung up and turned to her husband, her expression was grim. "Richard, Val's—"

Richard swallowed his bite of English muffin. "I know."

"You do? When did you find out?"

"Last night." Richard helped himself to another serving of eggs. "I ran into Ginger on my way home. She was just coming back from the Ewings'."

"You knew, and you didn't tell me!" Laura stared at her husband in surprise. It wasn't like him not to tell her neighborhood news—especially something as serious as this. True, she and Richard had had their troubled times when they had been virtual strangers sharing a household. But those times were over—weren't they?

"Why didn't you tell me?" she repeated.

"I guess I didn't want to upset you. Look, it may be nothing."

"Nothing!" Laura's eyes flashed with anger and fear. "Not according to Karen."

Deliberately, Richard took a sip of coffee before he replied. "Oh, Karen." He waved a hand dismissively. "Karen's probably got Val dead and buried already."

Laura leaned against the counter and stared at the man who sat so comfortably at their kitchen table. Was this unfeeling man her husband? No wonder he made such a good attorney—he looked at everything dispassionately, considering only facts, not people.

"That's a terrible thing to say."

"The surgery is merely precautionary." Richard cut a piece of bacon, speared it with his fork and chewed it carefully. "Could we talk about something else? This isn't my idea of the way to start our day."

"Okay." Laura sat down at the table and tried to eat her breakfast, but the food stuck in her throat. Val, her friend and neighbor; Val, who had done so much for her; Val, who had always been there when she needed her; Val was facing surgery. Laura's appetite disappeared completely.

Richard drained his coffee cup and looked at his wife. "I'm sorry. It is serious. But when I heard the news, the only thing I could think was, 'Thank God it's not Laura.' Awful, isn't it?"

Laura managed a faint smile.

"Avery residence."

"Laura, what's wrong? That's twice you've answered the phone that way. This is the Scooter Warren Agency, in case you haven't noticed." Marge's voice was joking, but there was no doubt that she was concerned.

"Nothing's wrong." Laura shook her head. "I'm just a little preoccupied." She looked down at the notes on her desk. She was supposed to be finding a house for a TV producer to rent for the summer months. The listings were spread in front of her, and she had opened a map to check their locations. But instead of looking at the street addresses, she had circled the location of every hospital on the map.

"Laura, line three for you," Marge called, "It's Val—"

Laura grabbed for the phone so quickly that she knocked over her cup of coffee.

"Hi, Val. How are you?" Her voice was full of concern, but as the caller replied, Laura's expression changed. "Oh, yes, Mrs. Middleton, I'm working on your house." It was just a business call—Valerie Middleton, not Val Ewing.

When she hung up the phone, Laura began to mop up the spilled coffee. She might as well go home. Maybe she'd do less damage there.

"Come into my office, please."

Laura dropped the stained paper towel in her wastebasket and looked up to see Scooter Warren standing in front of her desk. Just what she needed! He was sure to have another project for her. Why now, when she couldn't even handle something as simple as a cup of coffee? But Laura said nothing, merely gathered up a pad and pencil and followed him to his office.

Despite her frazzled nerves, she was a graceful figure as she walked toward the corner office. With her long hair carefully arranged in a twist and in her neatly tailored suit, Laura was the picture of the quintessential career woman. She was beautiful, but wise enough to tone down her looks so that she was not threatening to clients, and so she appeared attractive rather than stunning.

Scooter stood aside as she entered the office, then closed the door. Laura's eyes mirrored her surprise. This must be serious. Scooter rarely closed the door for anything less than a summit conference. Her concern grew when he took the seat next to her rather than his high-backed desk chair.

"Okay. What's wrong?" Scooter's voice was matter-of-fact.

"Nothing."

Scooter shook his head. "Try again. I'm not buying that one. You haven't been yourself all day. You sit there like you're in a fog; you forget you're even in the office; and you seem to be poisoning yourself with coffee."

"The last cup poisoned the desk." Laura smiled faintly, surprised that her boss had noticed so much. Marge always claimed that he was unaware of what was going on around him, that nothing short of an atomic bomb would get his attention.

"Well, I'm glad to see you can still laugh." He turned to face her. "Now, tell me what's wrong."

His dark eyes were concerned, and Laura found herself relaxing for the first time since Karen had called with the news. "A good friend of mine has cancer. She's in the hospital for surgery."

"And you feel guilty, because you can't help her."

She nodded, surprised at Scooter's depth of understanding. Although he had always been a good boss, demanding but fair, ready to turn an awkward situation into a joke, this was the first time Laura had realized that he was also a deeply compassionate man. "Val's so young and lively, and I can't bear the thought of her suffering."

"What kind of surgery?"

She explained Val's dilemma.

He lowered his eyes in sympathy. "That's one of the toughest. It's not just the physical trauma, either. There's a lot of emotional pain."

"That's what I'm worried about."

Laura continued speaking softly, confiding her fears for Val and Gary and their marriage. Sometimes Scooter answered her, offering words of comfort, but for the most part he let her talk without interrupting, knowing that merely vocalizing her fears would lighten them.

When her voice finally trailed off, Scooter stretched his arm along the back of the couch, encircled her shoulders and drew her closer to him. Laura came willingly, and they sat in silence for a few moments as she drew comfort from his touch. In the circle of Scooter's arms, she was safe. Her fears for Val had not disappeared, but they had diminished. She was no longer alone.

Laura barely felt the light kiss Scooter pressed on her hair.

Gary walked slowly from one end of the showroom to the other, stopping before each car to read the sticker. There was no reason for him to do so. He already knew which options were on every car, but he was filled with nervous energy, and this was one way of dissipating it.

When he reached the middle of the showroom, he paused at the red convertible, studying it from every angle. Then he slid behind the steering wheel, turned the key in the ignition and lowered the roof. His hands caressed the fine leather upholstery, and he breathed in the unmistakable new-car scent. It was a beautiful machine!

When he and Sid had ordered it, they had loaded it with options; anyone who'd pay the premium for a convertible would want the best stereo and the deepest-pile carpeting. But when the car arrived, it had been even more gorgeous than Gary had expected. It was the perfect car for Val.

Abruptly Gary scrambled out of the low-slung seat and closed the door with more force than necessary. He strode away from the convertible and out of the showroom, his mind whirling in pain.

Val! Beautiful, beautiful Val!

He'd hated leaving her at the hospital. Somehow, seeing her in that sterile hospital bed, framed by plain white sheets instead of the pretty prints and stripes she bought for their bed, had been the hardest part. Before that, even when they had been filling in the endless insurance and registration forms, it had seemed like a dream. A nightmare, really. But when Val had hung her clothes in the closet and climbed into the bed, it had suddenly changed from a dream into reality. There she was, his Val, and she was going to have surgery.

Gary wandered through the lot, mechanically checking each car to be sure it was locked.

What was he going to do? The doctor's words still echoed in his head. Val had blanched as Dr. Harper explained the details of the surgery, the changes it would bring about in her life. He hadn't tried to minimize them, but he had taken a positive approach, and Val had seemed to accept his words. It was Gary who had been unable to face them.

Val, beautiful Val, her smooth skin marred by an ugly scar, her body changed forever. Oh, how was he going to bear it? How could he look at her and not think of the awful thing that had been done to her? How could he pretend that nothing had changed? Gary leaned on the roof of a car and closed his eyes in despair.

A couple of minutes later he heard approaching footsteps but did not look up. Perhaps if he ignored whoever it was, they'd go away. But the footsteps drew closer, and the familiar scent of Abby's perfume filled his nostrils.

"Can a friend say she's sorry?" Abby asked, her voice husky with emotion. Val wasn't her favorite person, but Abby had been shocked when Sid had told her of the upcoming operation.

Slowly Gary turned around and shrugged. "Hi, Abby."

"Oh, Gary, I'm so sorry." Tears filled Abby's large violet eyes. "This shouldn't happen to anyone." She placed a carefully manicured hand on his arm, and her eyes beseeched him not to push it away.

He looked down at her. "All I can think about is Val and how much I love her. How can I ever live without her?"

"But Sid said—"

"Sid wasn't there. He doesn't know what the doctor said. Believe me, Abby, it's serious."

Abby tightened her grip on Gary's arm.

"I want to help you." Fleetingly, she thought of the other times she had tried to help Gary. She had even enlisted his brother J.R.'s help.

J.R., now there was a man. Handsome, powerful, rich. Unfortunately, he was also a man who had seen too much, who had seen through Abby's strategy and who knew that her motives were far from altruistic. Abby dismissed J.R. from her thoughts. He was thousands of miles away. What mattered was Gary, and he was here.

"Let me help you," she repeated.

But Gary turned away, brushing her hand from his arm. "No one can help," he said.

As he walked slowly away between the rows of cars, Abby studied him. Her eyes narrowed, and a feline smile crossed her face. Gary was wrong. *She* could help.

When Dr. Harper entered room 217, Val was sitting propped up by pillows, slowly twisting the hospital identification bracelet on her left wrist, while Gary paced from door to window and back again.

"Hello, doctor." Gary tried to keep his voice from trembling.

Dr. Harper nodded in greeting, then suggested that Gary sit down. Grasping Val's hand between both of his, Gary took the seat next to the bed.

"I've gotten the results of the tests," the

doctor spoke quickly, not wanting to pro-
long the Ewings' agony of waiting. "The
growth was lower down in the colon than
we had thought—at nine centimeters."

Val remained silent. It was Gary who
said, "That's not good, is it?"

"No." Dr. Harper looked down at the
charts. "At that position, it's hard to reach
because the pelvic bone is in the way. It's
difficult to reconnect the intestinal tissue."

Val said nothing. Only the tightening of
her hand within Gary's indicated that she
had heard the news and understood the
implications. She looked at the doctor for
a moment, then at Gary. Beneath his tan,
Gary's face was ashen. Val managed a
weak smile. It was meant to be reassuring, but it was Gary's undoing. His shoulders slumped and his head dropped as he
struggled against the weight of the news.

Dr. Harper continued, "The next step is
surgery. The sooner the better." He waited
until Gary raised his head again, then
looked slowly from one to the other.
"Unless you want a second opinion."

"A second opinion?" Val spoke for the
first time.

"What for? Is there any question?"

The doctor shook his head. "Not in my
mind. But a second opinion may reassure
you."

Gary looked at Val, his eyes searching
her face for a reaction. "Maybe we
should."

"No." Val's response was immediate, her voice tinged with anger. "I don't want any more examinations. No more tests. No more talk about centimeters. Let's get on with it."

There was a moment of silence before Dr. Harper spoke again. "We have consent forms for you to fill out." He looked at Val, encouragingly. "First, let me reemphasize that the odds are in your favor. I'm pretty sure I removed the entire malignancy before it spread." He directed his next words to Gary. "But you should be prepared for what may happen."

Gary shuddered, and the doctor looked at Val, his eyes filled with concern. She nodded slightly, as though to tell him not to worry, that she would take care of her husband.

Dr. Harper rose. "I'll ask one of the nurses to bring you some literature. Please read it carefully."

When the doctor's footsteps had faded away, Val turned to her husband. Poor Gary! He was taking this worse than she. She put her hand on top of his head and stroked it gently, comforting him as she would a child.

Gary found his wife smiling when he returned from the cafeteria. Her lunch tray had been cleared away, and the top of her bed was now covered with pamphlets.

"You should see this!" Val said, and laughed lightly, but her laugh was one of nervousness, not mirth.

"What?" Gary tried to keep his tone light. Val had enough to cope with without having him reveal how shaken he was by the doctor's prognosis.

"Look at this." She waved a brightly colored leaflet in Gary's direction. "It must be magic. This says I'll be able to scuba dive after the operation. Funny, I never could scuba dive before."

Gary forced himself to smile. How could she joke about it? Her life—no, their life—was about to change forever, and she could still laugh.

Val handed Gary one of the pamphlets. "You ought to read this." But he dropped it quickly as though it burned his fingers, and picked up a cassette instead. That, at least, didn't have pictures. "What's this?"

"It's some instructions."

Gary clutched the cassette. "I'll go home and get you the tape player," he said as he stood up.

"Honey, I'm sure the hospital has one. You don't have to go."

But Val was wrong. Gary had to go. He knew that if he stayed in that hospital room one more minute, he'd break. He had felt the tension building all morning. First there had been the scene with Abby in the used car lot. Then the doctor had given them the results of the tests. And

now Val was trying to pretend that everything would be normal. It wouldn't! And
being here just reminded him of how
abnormal it was going to be. He had to
get out.

"Look, I've got to make a few calls. I'll
see you later, okay?"

Gary tried to ignore the hurt expression
on his wife's face. Didn't she understand
that he couldn't stay? She tilted her face
up so that he could kiss her. A feeling of
revulsion swept through Gary as he
thought of the surgery, and he recoiled a
pace. Then, seeing the pain in Val's beautiful blue eyes, he leaned down and
kissed her gently.

Gary slammed the gearshift lever into
first and pushed his foot to the floor,
ignoring the angry squeal of the tires as
he left the parking lot. The sooner he got
away from that hospital, the better.

A few moments later, Gary was on the
freeway heading home. Traffic was lighter
than usual, and there were no highway
patrolmen in view. Nothing to stand
between him and Knots Landing, nothing
between him and home.

Gary pushed the accelerator toward the
floor. He had to get home. Maybe there
the nightmare would end. Maybe he
would finally waken and realize that it
had all been a dream, an awful dream.

As he turned into the cul-de-sac, Gary
leaned forward to push the electric

garage-door opener. He did not notice the figures in the neighboring yard.

Sid and Eric Fairgate were playing football. Sid took a couple steps back and threw a pass toward his son. And Eric, running backward to catch it, had only one thought: he was going to catch this one, he would not fumble again. His attention was so focused on the football, he didn't hear the car approaching.

The blue sedan shot forward as the garage door opened. Suddenly a figure ran onto the driveway. Gary leaned on the horn. Damn it! He slammed on the brakes and flung the door open.

"You little creep!" Gary shouted, swinging his fist at Eric. "I could have killed you!"

Eric jumped back to avoid the blow.

"Gary!" Sid shouted. He ran toward them, trying to put himself between his neighbor and his son.

As Sid and his son watched openmouthed, Gary Ewing stormed into his house.

Chapter Four
Friends and Family

"Mrs. Ward, Mrs. Ward, Johnny took my red crayon!"

"I did not!"

"She said I was ugly!"

"He didn't hang his knapsack on the right hook."

The cacophony of voices surrounded Ginger. Normally she didn't mind; in fact, she loved her pupils and found their minor squabbles almost amusing. Almost. But today was different. Today even the smallest disagreement annoyed her, and the children's voices, far from sounding sweet, seemed querulous and shrill. It was the sort of day when Ginger began to reconsider. Perhaps the old adage wasn't so wrong—perhaps children *should* be seen and not heard. In fact, maybe they shouldn't even be seen.

"All right, children," she said. "It's time

for art. Get out your coloring books."
Squeals of delight greeted her words. If
there was anything the children loved, it
was coloring. And, more importantly for
Ginger, it was an activity they could do
quietly, without her assistance.

When twenty-five heads were bent
intently over their desks, Ginger eased
herself into her chair and slid her feet out
of her shoes. These shoes had never hurt
before; why did they pick today of all
days to pinch? Probably, Ginger answered
herself, because today was "one of those
days."

The children murmured and whispered
among themselves and there was the
occasional sound of a dropped crayon, but
compared to the previous noise level, the
classroom was silent. Satisfied with what
she saw, her thoughts returned to the
problem that had been haunting her all
day: Val.

By now she should have the results of
the tests. Karen had reported that the doctor would have them by noon. Surgery
would be scheduled for the next morning.
That was why Karen had called Ginger
this morning, to suggest that she and the
other women from the cul-de-sac visit Val
this evening.

Oh, Val! Ginger closed her eyes as she
thought of the crisis her friend was facing.
Hadn't she gone through enough already?
Ginger knew that Val's life hadn't been an

easy one, but since she had come to Knots Landing, it had seemed to improve. And now! Now vibrant, chipper Val was seriously ill.

I wonder if I'd be as brave if I were facing that kind of surgery? Would I be able to smile? Would I be able to pretend that nothing was wrong, that it would all work out? Ginger shook her head. She didn't think so.

She slipped her shoes back on and walked around the classroom, looking at each student's work, praising the better efforts, helping the children who needed more attention.

As she returned to her desk, she felt a distinct kick. The baby was moving! In the earlier months when she had first felt movement, it had been the merest fluttering, a movement so slight she thought she had imagined it. But now there was no doubt about it. That kick to the ribs was no flutter.

Ginger smiled to herself and wondered if she would ever grow accustomed to the miracle of her child. Oh, the timing could have been better—she and Kenny had already been separated when she learned she was pregnant. But even knowing she would be a single parent, and fully aware of the problems that entailed, she had never once considered an abortion. One of those in a lifetime was more than enough.

She had been a teenager, barely more than a child herself, and her parents had been adamant that she was too young to bear and raise a child. At the time, the decision had seemed the right one. It was only afterward that the nightmares had started, dreams of the little girl—for she'd been convinced the baby would be a girl—playing in a sandbox or on a shiny new swing-set. Ginger would wake up in tears, convinced that she had destroyed her one chance at motherhood, her one chance to love a child. It was no coincidence that she had become an elementary school teacher. Here she was able to lavish her affection on an entire roomful of children.

But now, with this pregnancy, she was being given a second chance. And this time nothing would stop her. Not Kenny, not the difficulty of being a single parent, nothing.

"Mrs. Ward, look at my picture of the park."

The innocent request caught her completely off-balance. Ginger gazed at the page colored with purple leaves, red tree trunks and orange grass and suppressed a gasp.

"Very nice, Jerry," she said distractedly as Kenny's words echoed in her head: "A young couple, like us." *No, Kenny, they weren't like us. That woman could count on him. I could never count on you. That's one thing I learned, way before this baby was conceived.*

Ginger fixed a smile on her face. She didn't want to worry the children by appearing upset, but her thoughts were far from happy. When had it started? They had been so happy when they were first married, or so Ginger had thought. And then she had realized that not all of the business trips were necessary and that Kenny wasn't hurrying home because his traveling companions provided all the comforts of home.

When she first discovered that he was unfaithful, she had thought the pain was too much to bear. It had grown worse. For Kenny would come home, promising that this was his last affair, and Ginger would begin to hope again. Each time, though, she was disappointed, and each time, the pain had deepened. Finally, she had mustered every ounce of courage and told him to leave. Living alone might be hard, but it was better than living with a part-time husband.

The first few months had been easier than Ginger expected. The joy of her pregnancy occupied her thoughts, and her friends had been wonderful. Val and Karen had been there whenever she needed them, and Laura, busy Laura, often made room in her schedule to meet Ginger for dinner. The time had passed quickly, and if she missed Kenny, she had only to remind herself of the broken promises and the heartache.

She couldn't say when her feelings had started to change. Was it because Kenny seemed to be staying put in L.A.? Was it because the baby was becoming a real person, and she wanted it to have a father as well as a mother? Was it because Kenny seemed sincere? He'd even had tears in his eyes when he told her about the couple in the park. The old Kenny would have been too blasé to notice a pregnant woman, much less watch while she shared an intimate moment with her husband.

Was it possible that Kenny had changed? Was it possible that they had a chance together?

Gary ran as though pursued. He slammed the front door behind him, then stormed up the stairs two at a time, his feet pounding so hard that the staircase shook. It was only when he reached the bedroom that he stopped.

For a moment he stood still, and the only sound was the pounding of his heart. His eyes darted from one side of the room to the other. Although he and Val shared the entire house, this was the place that was theirs most of all. It was here that they spent their happiest moments. It was here that they shared their dreams.

The room was filled with Val. Her picture was on top of the bureau. Her slippers were next to the bed. Her scent was in the air. The room was waiting for her to walk back in. But she wouldn't.

Fury swelled in him. What right did fate have to do this to him? Nobody treated Gary Ewing this way!

His last fragile thread of control snapped. Gary lunged forward, his fury beyond all reason. In one swift movement, he reached the dressing table and swept his arm across its top, knocking the jars and bottles onto the floor. Shards of glass flew in all directions, and the air filled with the aromas of perfume, hand cream and nail polish. The crystal perfume stopper he had given Val for Christmas somehow survived the crash, but it lay spattered with pale green lotion as the perfume leaked slowly onto the floor.

Gary spun around. Spying the portrait of Val on the bureau, he grabbed it and hurled it to the floor; the silver frame bent and slivers of glass dug into the hardwood floor. He wanted no reminders, nothing at all.

Yanking drawers from the bureau, Gary dumped their contents onto the floor, then hurled them into the corner. And still he was not satisfied. He strode toward the bed, his face contorted with pain as he remembered the nights he and Val had shared there. Never again. He ripped the sheets from the bed, flinging them across the room as he had a fleeting image of Val in the hospital bed, looking young and defenseless.

"I can't!" he shouted. "I can't, I can't, I can't." It became a litany, and with each repetition, he hurled an object across the room or yanked a lamp from the wall, venting his rage in physical effort until the room was a shambles.

There was one more cord. Gary tugged at it, but it did not come loose. He tugged again. Tears of frustration rose to his eyes. It was such a small thing, and yet it defied him. Then, as Gary squinted, he saw that the cord was attached to the telephone.

Staring at the phone, Gary felt the anger drain from him, leaving utter desolation behind. He was going to lose Valene! He would be all alone!

Crumpling to the floor, he pulled the phone onto his lap, grasping the cord as though it were a lifeline. Slowly he dialed the number, a number that, no matter what had happened, he could never forget.

The phone rang three, four times, and still there was no answer. Oh, God! What if she wasn't home? She had to be! She could help him. She'd know what he should do. No one else would understand. No one else would care.

On the other end, a woman answered the phone.

At the sound of the familiar voice, Gary's sobs began again. "It's me, Mama."

His words were broken and his voice thick. "I can't do it. I can't. It's Val and she's sick and I can't help her." The rest of his words were incoherent, distorted by his sobbing.

Sid Fairgate motioned to his son. "Go into the house, Eric." The last thing he wanted was his child outside where he could be further exposed to Gary's fury.

What on earth was wrong? Sid thought he knew Gary better than anyone else in Knots Landing. After all, they weren't just neighbors; they worked together.

What had happened at the hospital to turn Gary into a raving lunatic?

"Gary!" Sid called, and rang the doorbell. There was no answer. He tried the knob, but the door was locked. "Let me in." The only response was the sound of shattering glass.

Sid banged on the door. "Open up!" What the hell was Gary doing in there? Sid heard splintering wood and the dull thud of objects hitting the floor. Good God, what was going on? Had Gary gone totally berserk?

Sid wedged his shoulder against the door, trying to force the lock. He had to get inside. God only knew what Gary would do next.

The door began to give as Sid continued to batter at it. With a final thrust, he pushed it inward. But as he rushed into

the Ewings' house, Sid felt a chill of fear
creep down his spine. The house was too
silent. Had Gary begun to drink? Sid had
helped Gary through the tail end of his
long battle with alcohol. Now Gary
attended A.A. regularly. Under the strain
of Val's illness, had he succumbed to the
temptation?

Moving quietly but quickly, Sid climbed
the stairs and entered the Ewings' bedroom.

The thuds and the sound of shattering
glass had suggested that the room would
be a mess, but they were inadequate
warning. The bedroom wasn't a mess; it
was a disaster area.

The room's condition was mirrored in
the man who sat in the middle of the
floor, his shoulders stooped in despair, his
eyes red-rimmed from weeping. He cra-
dled a telephone in his lap as he stared
sightlessly at the wall.

"Gary." Sid's voice was low and even.
He couldn't let Gary know how shocked
he was by his appearance. At this point,
that might be enough to drive him over
the edge.

Gary looked up, his expression dazed.
For a moment he stared at Sid, uncompre-
hending. Then he nodded.

Sid sank down on the heap of blankets
next to Gary. Thank God! There was no
sign of alcohol. Whatever else he had
done, Gary had not turned to drink.

The sound of brisk footsteps echoed on the stairs. Both men turned as they grew closer.

"Oh, my God!" Karen's dark eyes widened in shock.

Sid shook his head slightly, a silent warning to Karen to remain calm.

"It should have happened to me," Gary said, his voice choked with emotion. "To me, not her."

Sid put a hand on Gary's shoulder, trying to give him the support he so obviously needed.

"I heard that word, cancer; it was the loudest word I ever heard." Gary shrugged off his neighbor's hand.

Karen uttered a small cry of distress.

Gary looked up at her. "Val's spent more than half her life investing in a dream, her dream for me, and what have I done? I've run away, abandoned her, been somewhere else when she needed me . . ."

Karen couldn't bear the pain in his tone. "Not anymore," she said, her voice warm with compassion.

"Oh, no?" Gary shook his head. "Now I'm here. Lying to her, trying to pretend that all this doesn't matter." He looked from Karen to Sid, his blue eyes imploring them to understand. "And all I can think about is how much I love her."

"Then concentrate on that," Sid said firmly. They had to get Gary to focus on something positive, something to lift him from this depression.

"Concentrate?" Gary threw up his hands in a gesture of defeat. "When I concentrate, I see myself running from her again, the way I always ran from her. That's what I did today. She needed me at the hospital, and I ran away."

Sid stood up, then took Gary's arm and pulled him to his feet. "Listen to me, Gary. Take it one step at a time. That's the best you can do now." He waited until Gary met his eyes. "Today's step is to stay by Val's side and tell her how much you love her. Don't talk about the future. Don't even think about that yet. One step at a time."

"I told Val I'd be right back. She's expecting me at the hospital." Gary turned away from Sid and looked around the room, and from his expression it was clear that he was actually seeing it for the first time, that the damage was as shocking to him as it had been to Sid and Karen. He seemed unaware that he was responsible for the destruction.

Karen, who had been watching Gary carefully, anticipated his need. "We'll get the kids in to clean up the mess."

"Thanks." Just one word, but it was enough. Both Sid and Karen recognized the difference in Gary's voice. This was the old Gary. They exchanged a look of victory.

Gary glanced down at his crumpled clothes. "I've got to shave . . . clean up a little . . ."

Karen nodded. "Use our house," she suggested.

When Gary had left, she turned to Sid, her brown eyes sad. "He's not going to get through this one, Sid. It's too much for him."

Wordlessly, Sid nodded.

Chapter Five
Visiting Hours

"No more orchids for my love."

As the voice held the last mournful note, letting it fade slowly into silence, Kenny nodded. "That's it, Hank. You've got it." There was more than a hint of relief in his voice.

It had been a long morning. Fans might call Hank Baxter the hottest new country sound, but this morning he'd been only lukewarm. His normally mellow voice sounded strained, and it had taken twice as long as it should have to record "Orchids."

As the ninety-minute session stretched into hours, Kenny had been close to walking out. *Let Baxter find another recording studio!* But common sense, pressing bills and the memory of how good Hank Baxter's voice could be kept Kenny from exploding. Instead, he paced the floor, staring at the instruments and trying not to wince when the needle registered yet another crack in Baxter's tenor. But now it was done.

"Great job, Hank!" Kenny clapped the singer on the back. "It's gonna be platinum. I know it."

"Sure thing." Hank Baxter grinned as he wiped beads of perspiration from his forehead. "You know what I like about working with you?" He wadded the handkerchief and stuffed it back in his pocket. "You've got a first-class act here, and you won't let anyone get away with less."

It was Kenny's turn to grin. Hank's words were music to his ears. That was what he had tried to do—set up a studio that produced only top-quality recordings.

"Kenny."

He heard himself being paged. Kenny reached over and pressed a button on the intercom. "Yes?"

"Your wife called. She said not to interrupt you, that she'd call back at lunch."

The rush of terror that filled him was senseless, Kenny told himself. There was no reason to be alarmed. Ginger probably had a good reason for calling him. It was just that she never phoned during the day. When she needed to talk to him—and he had to admit that Ginger rarely initiated their conversations recently—she called at night. Why was she calling? Had something happened to the baby?

"Something wrong, man?"

Kenny looked at Hank Baxter, then shook his head. "No, nothing." Totally unaware that he was being rude, Kenny stalked to his office, closed the door with a snap and spent the next hour staring out the window, worrying.

When the phone rang, he grabbed it before the first ring was finished. "Is the baby okay ?" The words were out of Kenny's mouth before Ginger had a chance to do more than say hello.

"The baby?" Ginger chuckled. "He's fine. Just a little rambunctious today— been doing a lot of kicking. Why did you think something was wrong?"

"Because you never call me during the day."

There was a moment's silence. "You know it's hard for me to get away from class. And the only phone is in the teachers' lounge— not the most private of places."

"Look, Ginger, I'm not complaining." Kenny's pulse was returning to normal now that he realized the baby was fine. "I was just concerned when you called. I guess I jumped to conclusions and assumed it was something bad."

"Well, you were right." Ginger's voice was strained. "It is bad news, but not about the baby. It's Val. She's in the hospital."

Kenny listened while Ginger explained about Val's surgery. Worriedly, he ran a hand through his blond hair. "Can I go to the hospital with you? I'd like to see Val."

"Sorry, Kenny. I promised the girls I'd go with them. And then I have to go to the Lamaze class. It's my night to observe, and the class is right at the hospital. I'll go there after I see Val."

"But I could be with you."

"Sorry, Kenny, but no."

As he hung up the phone, Kenny stared around his office. God, he'd come a long way! In just a few years he had turned his dream into the reality of a successful recording studio. He no longer operated out of a single rented room in a neighborhood where artists feared to walk after dark without the protection of their Doberman pinschers. Instead he had a well-designed suite of offices and studios in a prestigious location. Envious people gave the credit to luck. Kenny knew his success was the result of hard work. But today, none of it seemed to matter.

He swiveled his chair to look out the window. It was another perfect California day. The sun was shining, and the smog level was low. If he craned his neck, he could see over the next row of buildings to the distant mountains that surrounded Los Angeles. Normally the view soothed him, reminding him how much he loved southern California. But today it was just a view.

What was wrong? It wasn't just Ginger's phone call, although he had to admit that he was shaken by the news of Val's illness. If there was anyone this shouldn't have happened to, it was Val. For Val, alone among his former neighbors, had always made Kenny feel welcome. It was as though she recognized his weaknesses but accepted them. And Val didn't take sides. He knew she was Ginger's friend, but even when he and Ginger had split up, Val had remained his friend, too. The rest of the women generally treated him as if he had climbed out from under some slimy rock. But Val was different. That was why it was so unfair that this was happening to her.

But it wasn't just Val's problems that were bothering Kenny. Slowly he paced from one end of the office to the other, trying to put his thoughts in order.

He'd been jittery for the past few days. When had it started? As he looked out the window, he remembered the day he had walked through the park in Santa Monica. Had that been the beginning? Had it been the sight of the pregnant woman that upset him, that crystallized his thinking about his child? Or had it started before that? Kenny didn't know. But he was sure of something else—he wanted that baby. He wanted to be with Ginger, to share their child's birth and to be there as the baby grew. And when Kenny Ward wanted something, he got it.

* * *

"Something tells me this isn't going to work." Karen looked at her neighbors and shook her head. She, Ginger, Laura and Abby were seated in the hospital cafeteria, picking at the trays of food in front of them.

"I've seen nicer dining spots, if that's what you mean," Abby groused as she poked at a piece of chicken with her fork.

"I don't think that's what Karen meant," Laura said. "Is it?" She looked at her neighbors. Ginger's pale complexion was even whiter than usual, and her green eyes seemed too large for her face. Karen's dark hair was tangled as though she'd forgotten to brush it. As for herself, Laura knew her eye makeup was smudged, and she'd forgotten to renew her blusher. Only Abby looked the same as ever—beautiful, glamorous, soignée. Val's illness was taking its toll on the cul-de-sac.

"We're supposed to be here to cheer Val up." Karen looked at the large clock on the wall, then checked her wristwatch. "We don't seem to be doing a great job of getting ready for it."

Ginger took a swallow of milk, then set her glass down. "How can anyone be cheerful in a place like this?"

As cafeterias went, it wasn't bad. The wood-grained Formica tables and imitation wood chairs kept it from looking institu-

tional, and there were framed floral prints
on the walls. The walls themselves were
painted a warm shade of peach, providing
the illusion of sunshine even at night.
Despite all the cozy touches, a pervasive air
of gloom hung over the room. There was no
escaping the fact that this was a hospital;
few of the visitors—and even fewer of the
patients—enjoyed being there.

"Think we should dance in and tell Val
jokes?" Abby asked, forcing a smile.

Karen shook her head. "No, but I was
hoping for something a little lighter than
the Four Horsemen of the Apocalypse."

Laura pushed a spinach leaf around her
salad bowl. "All I keep thinking is, why
Val? She's been through so much already."
She frowned, remembering the tragedies
that had haunted Valene's life.

"Why anybody?" Abby was pragmatic.
She cut a piece of her chicken and
chewed it slowly, thinking of Gary. What
would he do if something happened to
Val? Who would he turn to then?

Laura voiced the silent fear that each of
the women had confronted. "I don't
know what I'd do if it were me."

"You'd deal with it." Karen's words
were firm. She looked at the clock again.
Had the hands stopped? It felt as if they
had been sitting there for at least half an
hour, but according to the clock, it had
only been ten minutes.

"Not me. I couldn't deal with it."

Abby's violet eyes darkened as she thought of facing a major operation. "I couldn't stand it."

"I don't know." Once again it was Karen who offered reassurance. "You'd find strength you don't know you have."

Abby shook her head. "Not me." She sawed at the chicken cutlet.

"You can't deny that it changes things between a man and a woman," Laura said, her lovely face solemn. "Gary must be thinking about that." A frown crossed her face. How would Richard cope if she were the one having surgery? Would he rise to the occasion, or would he revert to his silent, distant moods? Unbidden, the memory of Scooter Warren's compassionate gaze flashed into Laura's mind. Scooter wouldn't desert a woman at a time like this. However dreadful it was, he would be there, supporting his wife, with enough strength for both of them.

"That's Gary's problem. I imagine Val feels the surgery is a small price to pay for her life." Karen's voice was cold, and the other three women looked at her in surprise. Why was Karen, normally so compassionate, talking this way?

Karen closed her eyes momentarily, remembering the scene she had witnessed in Gary and Val's bedroom. What would her friends say if they knew about that? What would Val do if she knew how her husband had fallen apart? Poor Val! She had so many worries; why did Gary have to add to them?

Abby pushed her tray aside. "God, this is depressing." She looked at the slender gold watch on her wrist. "It's seven o'clock. Let's get this over with." She stood up and walked toward the exit. Laura rose and followed her.

Karen reached for her handbag, but Ginger's voice stopped her.

"I can't do it. I can't go up there." Ginger's face was pale, and her green eyes seemed unnaturally bright. "I just can't." She looked at Karen, silently imploring her to understand.

"It's all right, Ginger," Karen said comfortingly, as though she were talking to her daughter. Her brown eyes filled with compassion. Ginger was so young. At times she seemed almost as young as Karen's daughter. This was probably her first experience with a serious illness.

"I want to go. I know I should go. But I can't." Ginger looked down at her stomach. "Val wanted a baby, you know that, Karen. How can I go in there with this stomach sticking out a mile, a reminder that I'm pregnant and she's not? And worse than that, she's sick." A shudder shook Ginger's slender shoulders. "Karen, I'm scared. I guess I'm just weak."

Karen reached across the table and touched Ginger's hand. "No, you're not. You're human."

* * *

Val clutched the pillow to her chest and inhaled deeply. She wiggled her toes, then exhaled quickly and coughed three times.

"What are you doing?" Gary, entering the hospital room, stopped and stared at his wife. He was clean-shaven and his hair was still faintly damp from the shower.

Val smiled. "These are breathing and coughing exercises. After the operation, I'm supposed to wiggle my feet to keep the circulation going, and I cough to clear my lungs."

She was amazing, this wife of his. Here she was facing major surgery, and her tone was as matter-of-fact as if she were telling him about a new laundry detergent. What had he ever done to deserve someone as wonderful as Valene? "You're too much."

"And you know what else?" Val announced. "I've made a promise to myself. After this is all over, I'm going to take the plunge: College—full-time."

Gary seemed surprised. "But you're already taking some courses."

"I know." She shrugged. "But I'm talking about really digging in. Studying for a career. I've never really focused my talents on any one thing. It's about time that I decided what to do with my life," she said with a laugh.

There was a knock on the door, and Karen's dark head appeared. "Can we come in?"

"Sure."

Karen, Abby and Laura entered the room. Gary moved to the corner and gestured toward the chair next to Val's bed.

"How's the patient?" Karen asked, keeping a cheerful tone as she looked from Val to Gary. He was still pale, and she could see that his breathing was irregular, as if he were trying to control it but not quite succeeding. "Want to get something to eat?" she suggested to him. "The Three Musketeers here will hold down the fort." She gestured to Laura, Abby and herself.

"Thanks." Gary turned quickly and left the room.

There was a moment of silence as the three women looked at Val, no one sure how to begin.

"No wonder you chose this place. I just saw a couple of the interns."

Karen winced. How like Abby! Here they were, supposedly to boost Val's spirits, and the only thing Abby could think about was men.

Val laughed, but it sounded shallow. "All I've seen are nurses and more nurses. And all *they* do is take my blood pressure."

"Just make sure they give it back," Karen quipped.

Val looked at her uncomprehendingly.

"It was a joke," Karen explained. "Once when Diana was little and she was sick, Sid asked her if she had a temperature. She said, 'No, Mommy took it.'"

Still Val did not smile.

"Okay, so I can't tell jokes." Karen walked over to the dresser and studied the cards propped against the flowers arranged there.

"You look okay." It was Laura's turn to try to cheer Val. "How's the food?"

"It's fine. I'm fine. A little nervous, I guess." Val looked at the pile of leaflets on the table next to her. "I'm not too worried. Only . . ."

Karen turned, hearing a different note in Val's voice, a hint of desperation. "Only what?"

Val tossed the pillow aside. "I'm worried about Gary. I've tried so hard to help him. I never wanted to add to his worries."

"Don't be silly." Karen moved quickly to the bed and looked down at Val. "You haven't done anything. I'm sure he doesn't feel that way." Karen hoped her words sounded sincere. Val knew her husband so well. It was almost as though she had been in their bedroom that afternoon and had seen the damage he had done in his rage.

"I know he doesn't." Val's voice was a little stronger, and she brushed a strand of blond hair away from her face. "He wishes this was happening to him so I wouldn't have to go through it."

Abby, who had been looking out the window, turned toward Val. "Gary's strong," she said confidently. "He'll be terrific, no matter what."

Karen was silent. The memory of Val's belongings lying shattered on the floor of her bedroom was all too vivid.

There was no doubt where the couples were going. If the women's rounded bellies weren't sufficient announcement, the pillows they and their husbands carried offered the final clue. The small sign on the door stating that this was the room for the Lamaze class was entirely superfluous.

Ginger walked purposefully along the corridor. She had read the book and practiced the exercises, but this was the real thing. Tonight she was going to see a Lamaze class in action. And, if she was lucky, it would keep her from thinking about Val and her ordeal. Focusing, that's what the Lamaze people called it. That's what she would try tonight. She would focus on pleasant thoughts, thoughts of her baby, and try to block out the nightmare of Val's illness.

Ginger rounded the corner and stopped abruptly. "What are you doing here?" she hissed.

Kenny straightened up from his relaxed

position against the wall and took a step toward her. "I'll fill in for Val." Seeing Ginger shake her head, he continued, "Just for tonight."

What was he doing here? she wondered. Wouldn't the man ever give up? And why now, when her nerves were so on edge from worrying about Val? "Val has nothing to do with this," Ginger said coldly. "I'm only observing."

"But Val was coming with you," Kenny pointed out. "I'll take her place."

Kenny's suggestion was perfectly reasonable. But suddenly Ginger's nerves, which had been strung as tight as the guitar Kenny used to play, snapped.

She placed one fist on her hip and faced Kenny squarely. "You will not take her place or any other place in my life!" Ginger shouted, her clear voice raised in anger. "Valene is upstairs about to undergo major surgery, and you use her pain to try and wheedle your way back into my life!"

As her words penetrated, Kenny's face in turn was suffused with anger. "Do you really believe that?"

"Yes, I really do."

Kenny looked at Ginger steadily for a moment. Then he spoke slowly, choosing his words carefully. "You know, Ginger, if that's what you think of me, maybe you're right." He looked at her waistline and an expression of pain crossed his face. "Maybe we shouldn't be married. Maybe we shouldn't even be friends."

He turned and walked away, leaving Ginger gazing after him with a startled look on her face. Slowly she turned away and entered the classroom.

The women were lying on the floor, their heads and knees propped up with pillows, their coaches kneeling next to them. Ginger was surprised to see that a third of the women were accompanied by female coaches. One coach, she guessed, was the pregnant woman's mother. Another, judging from the resemblance, was a sister. Ginger had been worried that she and Val would seem out of place in the class, that all the other coaches would be male. It seemed her concern was needless.

"We're going to try a sixty-second contraction," the instructor announced. "Everyone ready?"

As Ginger watched, a couple of the men touched their wives' cheeks gently, and one bent over to whisper something. She remembered the couple Kenny had mentioned seeing in the park. A man like that would be with his wife during the birth, encouraging her through each stage of labor.

"Contraction begins." The teacher clicked her stopwatch. "Take a cleansing breath. Relax. Focus." She began to walk from one couple to another, checking their progress.

"Make sure they're relaxed." At the instructor's direction, the coaches touched the women's arms, shoulders and legs, murmuring encouraging words.

"Contraction getting stronger." As though they were one, all the women began to breathe more quickly. "Stronger." And their breathing became even shallower as the women prepared for active labor.

Ginger walked around the perimeter of the room, watching the couples. The pregnant women were relaxed, concentrating only on the imaginary contraction, knowing that these exercises were important in preparing them for the actual birth. But what surprised her was the involvement of the coaches. She had assumed they had almost a spectator's role, but she was wrong. The coach was an integral part of the labor process.

Ginger studied the expressions on the coaches' faces. Was it her imagination, or were the men more involved? Was it because this was their baby, too, that they seemed to care more deeply than the other coaches?

The instructor clicked her stopwatch again. "Contraction over. Take another cleansing breath. Close your eyes. Relax."

The man who had whispered in his wife's ear at the beginning of the exercise pressed a light kiss on her forehead and flashed her a congratulatory smile.

Feeling more alone than she had in years, Ginger fled from the classroom.

She punched the button for the elevator, then changed her mind and headed for the stairs. As she walked, the image of the Lamaze class replayed in her mind, and a pang of jealousy swept through her. Those couples had something so precious! There had been a sense of sharing, of happiness and love. Those men and women had a commitment to each other and to their unborn children. Oh, why couldn't she have that, too?

Ginger reached the lobby and started toward the entrance, then stopped abruptly. She knew what she had to do. Quickly she turned and walked to the elevator.

She guessed that he would still be there. And he was. When she walked into the cafeteria, Ginger saw the two men sitting in the far corner, coffee cups on the table between them. With a determined step, she approached them. This wasn't going to be easy, but she knew it was the right thing to do. There was so much at stake—three lives, in fact.

"Is Val okay?" Ginger kept her eyes on Gary, although she was acutely aware of the other man.

"She's in good spirits."

"Give her my love." The words were mechanical, almost a reflex, something to say as she mustered her courage. For these next words were going to be the hardest she had said in a long time.

She swallowed, then turned slightly to speak to the other man. "Kenny?" Her voice was hesitant.

He looked up, his eyes questioning.

Slowly Ginger held out her hand. "We need you," she said.

Kenny rose from his seat and took Ginger's hand in his. His eyes searched her face, trying to decide what this meant, afraid to assume too much. But she met his gaze, and her smile was genuine.

"We need you," she repeated.

With a swift gesture, Kenny put his arm around Ginger's shoulders and led her from the cafeteria.

Gary watched them go, a pained expression on his face.

Chapter Six
Ties That Bind

The room was dark except for the flickering images on the television screen; the only sounds were the actors' voices and the tinny laughter of the studio audience. The show was the season's comedy hit, a program guaranteed to make even Ebeneezer Scrooge laugh. But Val Ewing gazed at it without a smile. Her eyes were focused on the screen; her thoughts were miles away.

Gary. What was he doing? When Karen had suggested that he go out for supper, he had seemed almost pathetically grateful to escape. Val knew that he was uncomfortable in the hospital. He didn't like being around sick people in general, and when the patient was his wife—well, it was no wonder he had wanted to escape. But that had been more than an hour ago. Where was he now?

A frown creased Val's face. She was the one who was facing surgery, but it was Gary who was suffering the most. If only there were some way she could help him!

The door opened, and Val looked at it expectantly. Gary was back! But although the figure that stood outlined in the door was familiar, it was not Gary. The build was similar, but this man had dark hair, not her husband's straw-blond shade.

"Bobby!" Val's voice trembled slightly as she called out his name. "Bobby Ewing, what are you doing here?"

"I should ask the same question of you." His Texas drawl was as pronounced as ever, and Val felt a surge of homesickness as her brother-in-law moved swiftly to her side and pressed a kiss on her cheek. She loved California and had never regretted moving to Knots Landing, but there were times when she wished she were back in Dallas—especially since Lucy was there.

"Oh, Bobby, it's wonderful to see you." Val turned on the bedside light and looked at him. His face was tanned from hours in the Texas sun, and he carried the familiar ten-gallon hat in his hand. Bobby hadn't changed one iota. It was so good to see him!

Val's gaze moved from Bobby to the door, a question in her eyes. Had he come alone, or had he brought her?

"Lucy?" she asked with a tremor in her

voice. Had her daughter come with him?

In response, Bobby grasped her hand. "Mama didn't think you'd want Lucy to know yet."

Val swallowed hard, fighting back the tears. "No, I don't," she admitted slowly. She had dreamed for so long of being reunited with her daughter—but not from a hospital bed, especially not when she was facing surgery and an uncertain future. That was no way to start a new chapter in their lives. No, when Lucy came back—and Val refused to believe that she would not come back—it would be a festive occasion. Miss Ellie was right in not sending her now.

"You look pretty well," Bobby said, his eyes examining Val's face and then glancing around the room. "This place looks like a subdivision of a florist's shop. Is there a single flower known to mankind that isn't on display here?" He grinned, hoping to bring a smile to Valene's face. Although he had told her she looked well, he had lied. Val was pale under her light tan, and her eyes were ringed with dark circles. Worse yet, there was a listlessness about her that Bobby had never seen before.

"Well, I did hear about this rare flower that blooms only in the snows of Tibet," Val said, chuckling. No matter what had happened in the past, she had always been able to count on Bobby. Why, he had even come with her and Gary when they first moved to Knots Landing.

Val smiled, remembering the moving van filled with Miss Ellie's cast-off furniture and how she had gradually replaced it with items she and Gary liked. When she had talked to Bobby, she had told him about the new furnishings, and they had shared more than one laugh about the demise of the fringed lampshade, a piece so hideous that she and Gary had relegated it to the attic immediately. Yes, Bobby was the best of brothers-in-law.

A sudden thought assailed Val. How had Bobby known she was in the hospital? She hadn't called him or anyone at Southfork. It had all happened too suddenly for her to tell the family. So, why was Bobby here?

"How'd you find out?" she asked, watching Bobby's face carefully. If there was one thing she knew about Bobby Ewing, it was that he couldn't lie to her.

Bobby looked at the floor, his unease clearly visible. "Gary called Mama," he said. Normally glib, Bobby stumbled over his words as he tried to explain. "She's pretty broken up over it and . . ."

There was no need for him to say more. Val knew from Bobby's distress exactly what had happened. So Gary had called Southfork, reached out to his family.

"Was he hysterical?" she asked.

Bobby studied the hat he held as

though the secrets of the universe were inscribed on the hatband. He said nothing.

"And she couldn't stand that," Val finished. She knew how the phone call would have distressed Miss Ellie.

Bobby raised his eyes to Valene's. "Mama went through this herself—something like it."

Val nodded. "I know." She remembered Miss Ellie's mastectomy and how deeply it had affected the whole family. That was, she knew, part of the reason that Gary was finding her own illness so difficult to accept. It shouldn't happen twice, not to two people so close to him. "Gary shouldn't have burdened his mama like that," she said.

When Val looked at Bobby, she saw compassion and love mingled in his eyes. That was her undoing. Suddenly her composure crumbled, and the tears began to roll down her cheeks. Ever since Dr. Harper had told her the results of the tests, she had forced herself to be optimistic, to think only about the odds in her favor, to smile and pretend nothing was wrong. She hadn't admitted the truth to anyone: not Gary, not Karen, not even herself. She had put on an award-winning performance, but now the act was over. With Bobby there was no need to pretend.

"Oh, Bobby, I'm so scared," she sobbed.

Bobby perched on the bed beside her and put his arm around her shoulders. The poor kid! She was a grown woman, the mother of a teenager, but at this moment Valene seemed no older than Lucy. She looked young and defenseless, and Bobby's heart went out to her.

"Don't tell Gary, but I'm awfully scared," she gasped, resting her head on his chest, trying to calm her breathing as she listened to the steady beating of his heart.

Bobby spoke slowly. "Nobody can tell you not to be scared. What you're facing is terrifying. Surgery is scary, and only a fool would deny that. You're not a fool, Valene. Far from it." His words were calm and even, and his tight embrace revealed his quiet strength.

Val sobbed for a few moments, then reached for a tissue. When she had wiped her eyes, she looked up at him. "Do you know everything?" Her voice cracked on the last word. "All the things that could happen?"

He nodded. "I spoke to the doctor." He patted her shoulder reassuringly. There was no need for her to explain. He knew that her composure was fragile, that having to describe her operation would be more than she could handle right now.

Finally, Val's breathing returned to normal. "I don't want to die," she said, her blue eyes filled with dread.

Bobby was prepared for this. "Then don't." He fixed his eyes on Val's, willing her to listen to him. "If you won't let yourself, you won't."

He spoke with confidence, and somehow Val trusted him even more than she had Dr. Harper. The doctor had assured her that the surgery would be successful, but she had not fully believed him. Even though she had read all the pamphlets with their emphasis on a nearly normal life, she had not really accepted them. What had been indelibly etched on her brain was the consent form she had signed, absolving the doctor and the hospital in case . . . Val shook her head. She wouldn't think about that. Instead, she would concentrate on Bobby's words. Somehow, they were easier to accept than those of the so-called experts.

She looked around the room, her eyes resting on the bouquets of flowers and the elaborate planters that covered most of the flat surfaces. She was silent for a few minutes. Then, compelled, she blurted out the fear that haunted her even more than the thought of death, the worry that was so real she had been afraid to voice it.

"I know Gary won't love me . . . if . . ." She could not complete the sentence. Val looked almost fearfully at Bobby, wondering if he was shocked by her words.

But he was not. "If you're alive, you're whole," he said, calmly but firmly, and turned to face Val fully. "You'll see that soon." The force of his words began to penetrate the haze of fear that had surrounded her. "Gary will, too."

"No, he won't." Val wanted badly to believe Bobby. There was nothing she wanted more than to believe that her husband would continue to love her, no matter what happened, no matter what the result of the surgery was. But she knew Gary, and her doubts remained.

"He will, Valene. I promise you that." Bobby's assurance banished some of Val's doubts. Bobby was Gary's brother, after all; he knew him as well as she did. If Bobby said everything would be all right, there was a good chance it would be. She wanted so desperately to believe that. And so she did.

Val offered Bobby a tremulous smile. "I'm glad you came," she said.

For the second time that day, the large blue sedan raced along the freeway, heading for Knots Landing. But this time, the driver did not honk his horn at motorists who happened to be obeying the speed limit, nor did he cut angrily in front of the inevitable car filled with tourists gawking at the sights. Instead, he drove courteously.

Gary pulled into the parking lot at Knots Landing Motors, flung open the car door and sprinted inside.

It was still there.

"Sid!" he bellowed as he raced to his desk, rummaging in the deep drawer for the camera he kept there. "Sid!"

"What's wrong?" Sid stood in the doorway, his dark eyes filled with concern. "Has something happened to Val?"

Gary grinned. "You could say that. She's about to become the proud owner of that red convertible. I came back to take a picture of it and to warn you that if you value your life, you won't sell it to anyone."

"Sure thing." Sid noted Gary's animation. This was a far different man from the one he had seen this afternoon. Thank God! That stranger was one he never wanted to meet again. This was more like the old Gary Ewing.

Gary fitted a flashcube onto the camera and walked back to the showroom. Then, after carefully considering the angle, he photographed the flashy sportscar that he had admired ever since it arrived. This was the perfect car for Valene. She had never complained about the secondhand wagon she drove. It was reliable transportation, and Val insisted that was all she needed. But the convertible was a classy car, and Val was a classy lady. They belonged together.

As he strode back to his own car, Gary heard a feminine voice calling his name.

"Hi, Abby," he said, slowing his pace only slightly.

Abby moved toward him quickly, her crimson dress swirling about her legs, her blond hair bouncing slightly. She reached Gary as he opened the door.

"I'm so glad to see you," she said. "I've been so worried about you. I wanted you to know that if there's anything I can do for you—anything at all—I will." Her violet eyes opened wide and she tipped her head back slightly, her smile promising far more than simple help. The long lines of her slender throat and the scent of her perfume were enough to set a man's pulse racing. But tonight Gary Ewing was immune.

"Thanks," he said, sliding behind the steering wheel. A moment later he was headed for the freeway.

It was probably silly of him—he certainly couldn't afford the car, not even with the generous discount Sid allowed him. But he wanted Val to have it.

It was hard to explain why he felt that way. Somehow, seeing Kenny and Ginger together had crystallized his feelings. It looked like they were once again going to be together, and that seemed right. It was right that he and Val should be together, too, but it had been too long since he had shown her how important she was to him. True, the car was only a gesture, but Val would recognize it as his way of saying "I love you." Gary hurried back to the hospital, anxious to tell Val about her new car.

"Hi, sweetheart," he called as he

opened the door to Val's room. But as he entered, he saw that she was not alone. A man was sitting next to Val, his arm wrapped protectively around her shoulders. Gary stopped short.

"Bobby?" he said. What was he doing here? "Did Mama . . . ?"

His brother rose quickly to face him. "Sit with your wife now," Bobby said, his voice emotionless. "We'll talk tomorrow." He kissed Val's cheek again, then walked to the door. As he passed Gary, he said, "I'll be back in the morning."

Val looked confused. Was there the hint of a threat in Bobby's voice?

Gary moved to his wife's side and kissed her tenderly. "Val, honey," he began, reaching into his pocket for the pictures. Then he caught sight of the tears rolling down Valene's face.

"What's wrong?" The terror that he had kept at bay threatened to overwhelm him. Val never cried. Something must be horribly wrong. Had the doctor come back? Had he found something else wrong?

"Oh, Gary." Val began to twist her wedding ring, and her sobbing intensified.

"Darling, what is it?"

Even when he put his hand under Val's chin and raised her face, she would not meet his eyes. She just kept twisting her ring and sobbing. A cold dread swept through Gary. He was going to lose her. He knew it.

"Please tell me what's wrong," he begged. "I've got to know."

Finally Val raised her eyes to his. "They won't let me wear my ring into surgery," she blurted out, and her sobs continued.

Was that all? Gary almost smiled in relief, but he caught himself in time. This was obviously important to Val. He mustn't belittle her fears. He drew her into his arms and held her close. "It'll be all right," he promised.

"But I've never taken my ring off, not once in all the years we've been married." Val's voice was plaintive. "I don't want to take it off now. I'll feel like we're not married anymore."

Gary blinked, hoping Val didn't see the tears that filled his eyes. "Val," he said, his voice thick with emotion, "you're my wife, ring or no ring. Nothing is going to change that."

Slowly, she nodded.

The next morning, when the orderly came to wheel her to the operating room, Val began to cry softly. She looked up at Gary, her blue eyes red-rimmed with tears. He tried to smile reassuringly, but his lips wouldn't curve upward. Instead, he managed a short nod.

Never taking her eyes from Gary's, Val slid her wedding ring from her finger. "Take care of it for me, please, honey."

He slipped it into the breast pocket of

his shirt, feeling tears begin to well in his eyes. "It'll be right here, next to my heart," he said, and his voice was husky with unshed tears.

Val smiled weakly, but she gripped her husband's hand as she was wheeled down the corridor. "I'm not really afraid," she said, not certain whether she was trying to convince herself or Gary.

"Neither am I," he lied.

When they reached the elevator, Gary bent down and kissed his wife. "I love you," he said.

As the elevator doors closed behind her, he shut his eyes in pain. God! How was he going to handle this?

Gary was certain that if surgery lasted one more minute, he'd wear a track in the linoleum floor. It seemed as if he had been pacing from one end of the waiting room to the other for days. He'd counted every tile on the floor and the ceiling, anything to make time pass.

The clock must have stopped, for it said that only half an hour had elapsed since he had left Val at the elevator doors. Dr. Harper had warned him that the operation would take two to three hours, and after that, Val would be in the recovery room for another hour or two. Oh, how was he going to last that long?

At the unmistakable sound of boots in the hallway, Gary turned around. "Thanks for coming," he greeted his brother.

But Bobby was not in the mood for polite conversation. "That was some phone call you made to Mama."

Gary, whose memories of the telephone call and that whole afternoon were hazy at best, nodded resignedly. "Sorry about that." What could he say? He wasn't proud of calling Mama, wasn't proud of anything he had done that afternoon. But he didn't remember what he had said, so how could he apologize?

"Better now?" Bobby's voice softened as he noted the confusion on his brother's face. He couldn't blame Gary for being himself. He could be angry with him, and—Lord knew—the family frequently was. But he couldn't really blame him. Gary was family, and he was lovable, even if he was occasionally weak and unreliable.

"I'm not crazy, if that's what you mean," Gary answered.

"That's not what I mean." As Bobby remembered the hurt his mother had endured and the pain on Val's face the night before, his anger grew. He balled his right hand into a fist and slammed it into his left hand. "I want to know if you're better. Have you pulled yourself together? Do you know what you're up against? Are you ready for it?"

Gary stiffened. "Don't preach to me, Bobby."

"Are you better, or aren't you?" his brother demanded.

Gary walked to the window and looked out at the parking lot. That was the question, and it wasn't just Bobby who was asking it. "I don't know," he said in a low voice.

In three quick strides, Bobby joined him at the window. "You don't have much time to find out," he said. "If you're going to sit here and wait this out, you'd damn well better know that you're going to be able to handle the outcome—whatever that is."

"Well, I don't know if I can handle it. How can I know?" Gary's tone was defiant. "Would you know?" he asked, still staring out the window.

"Damned right I'd know," Bobby replied instantly. "I'd grit my teeth and clench my fists and rail against fate, but I'd be ready for whatever came through that door." Bobby looked at Gary, his gaze like steel. "I couldn't live with myself if I broke down when the woman I loved needed me to be strong for her."

Gary stood silently, thinking about his brother's words. Bobby was right. But he made it sound easy when it wasn't. "Tell me how not to break," he said, looking imploringly at his brother.

"I'll tell you how not to break the way I told Val how not to die—don't."

Gary turned back to the window,

unwilling to face Bobby, filled with a sense of despair. "I can't handle the worst," he confessed.

Bobby grabbed his shoulder and jerked him around so that they were once again face to face. "The worst is if she dies," he said firmly.

Gary would not meet Bobby's eyes. Instead, he pulled away and began to pace the floor.

Bobby walked beside him, fitting his steps to Gary's. "You know that, don't you, Gary?" he insisted. "Dying is the worst thing that can happen to Val."

But he got no response.

Bobby raised his voice slightly. "Tell me you know that death is the worst possibility," he commanded.

Softly, like a child reciting by rote, Gary said, "It's the worst."

"I don't believe it!" Bobby's voice was filled with disgust, and he stopped abruptly. "You'd rather have your wife die than survive with a colostomy!"

Gary's shoulders sagged, and he returned to the window, pressing his face to the glass. Watching him, Bobby was filled with sadness. Poor, weak Gary! He'd never change. God help Valene!

"I was just a kid when you left," Bobby told his brother, "but I remember Mama and Daddy talking about you."

Gary turned slightly, and Bobby continued, hoping to shock some sense into him. "Daddy'd say you didn't have the Ewing guts. Mama'd say thank goodness for that, you had the Southworth gallantry, and that was much better. She thought guts were low-grade courage, but gallantry was courage with grace."

Although that had got Gary's attention, Bobby could tell that he wasn't really reaching him. As his brother once again faced him, Bobby's voice became cold and harsh. "It turns out that you don't have any sort of courage at all. That's why Mama didn't come. She heard it in your voice, and she couldn't stand to come here and see it for herself. You're nothing but a coward, Gary Ewing."

Gary stood for a moment staring at his brother. Then, without a word, he strode from the room.

Soaps & Serials™ Fans!

★ Order the *Soaps & Serials*™ books you have missed in this series.

★ Collect other *Soaps & Serials*™ series from their very beginnings.

★ Give *Soaps & Serials*™ series as gifts to other fans.

...see other side for ordering information

You can now order previous titles
of *Soaps & Serials*™ Books by Mail!

Just complete the order form, detach, and send together
with your check or money order payable to:

Soaps & Serials™
120 Brighton Road, Box 5201, Clifton, NJ 07015-5201

Please circle the book #'s you wish to order:

(A) The Young and
The Restless
1 2 3 4 5 6 7 8 9 10
11

(B) Days of Our Lives
1 2 3 4 5 6 7 8 9 10
11

(C) Guiding Light
1 2 3 4 5 6 7 8 9 10
11

(D) Another World
1 2 3 4 5 6 7 8 9 10
11

(E) As The World Turns
1 2 3 4 5 6 7 8 9 10
11

(F) Dallas™
1 2 3 4 5 6 7 8 9 10
11

(G) Knots Landing™
1 2 3 4 5 6 7 8 9 10
11

Each book is $2.50 ($3.50 in Canada).
Total number of books
circled_____ × price above = $ _____

Sales tax (CT and NY residents only) $ _____

Shipping and Handling $ _____.95

Total payment enclosed $ _____
(check or money orders only)

Name_____

Address _____ Apt#_____

City _____ State _____ Zip _____

Telephone (_____)_____
AREA CODE

KL 11

Chapter Seven
The Verdict

"Cellular chemistry? Are you sure that's what you want to major in?" Karen's dark eyes opened wide as she looked at the circled item on the page in front of her.

Diana laughed. "No, Mom. This is Derek's catalogue. He's the one who's going to be the chem major." She chuckled again. "Can you picture me in a college-level chemistry class? Me, who barely passed basic chem? No, thanks."

Diana's room was in its usual disastrous condition. With clothing and assorted possessions strewn over every available surface, it looked like a garage sale after a busload of eager shoppers had pawed through the merchandise.

Karen tried to ignore the chaos. At first, when Diana had entered this stage, Karen had despaired. But Sid, ever practical Sid, had convinced her that that was why doors

were invented. As long as Diana contained
the whirlwind within her room and kept the
door closed, Karen and Sid would not inter-
fere. So far the arrangement had worked. It
was only occasionally that Karen let the confusion bother her. She turned her attention
back to her daughter.

"Have you talked to the guidance coun-
selor about colleges?" she asked.

Diana wrinkled her nose. "Talk to
Cracker?"

Karen looked blank. "Cracker?"

"Her name's really Miss Graham,"
Diana explained, her tone slightly patron-
izing. "Graham cracker. Get it?"

Suddenly Karen was reminded of her
attempt to cheer Val and the way her joke
had fallen flat. Val! How was she? She
looked at her watch. The surgery would
be over soon.

"Thinking about Val?" There was no
laughter in Diana's voice now. "It was this
morning, wasn't it?"

Karen nodded.

"Do you think she'll be okay?" Diana
looked directly at her mother, her expression reflecting her concern.

"The doctor says she has a good
chance," Karen replied. "Beyond that, I
don't know. All surgery involves risks."
She watched Diana, trying to gauge her
reaction. A week ago, she probably would
have lied to Diana, minimizing the seriousness of Val's operation, sugar-coating

reality. But the past few days had changed that. Diana had heard her parents discussing Val's condition; she had seen the damage Gary had done to his house; she had been drawn into the crisis that was affecting the entire cul-de-sac, not just Val and Gary Ewing.

"What is this going to do to Gary?" Diana asked.

"I don't know," Karen admitted. "Your father said he seemed a lot better last night." She shifted on the chair and looked out the window. "Did you hear that he's buying Val a new car?"

Diana frowned. "Why? Is he trying to bribe her to live?"

Diana was definitely her child! That had been Karen's instinctive reaction, too, when Sid told her about the red convertible. But Sid had pointed out that Gary found it difficult to express his feelings verbally. To him, the car was a symbol of his love, a way of telling Val how important she was to him.

"Do you suppose she'll let me drive it?" Diana asked.

Karen smiled. There was still plenty of teenager left in Diana, despite the drama of the past few days. "I imagine so," she said.

Looking at her watch for the twentieth time in as many minutes, Karen bit her lip. How was Val doing? *Please, God, don't make Val suffer.*

"What's wrong, Mom?" Diana sensed her mother's tension.

"I'm worried, too," she admitted. Then, immediately practical, she added, "And the best thing when you're worried is to think of something else. Something nice."

"There's Ginger's baby," Diana volunteered.

Eagerly Karen clutched at the change of topic. "We ought to plan a shower for her. Just a small one. We'll invite all the women on the cul-de-sac."

"Can I come?" Diana asked.

"Of course. You're one of the women."

It was, Karen reflected, no exaggeration. In just a few days, Diana seemed to have matured. Perhaps some good had come out of Val's illness.

Laura Avery looked at her watch. She was late this morning, but that wasn't what bothered her. One of the good things about being a realtor was the flexible hours. Except for the days when she had call duty, she didn't have to go into the office at all. But Laura was a creature of habit, and working regular hours made her feel more professional. This morning, however, she clearly wasn't going to reach the office by nine.

Laura looked at her watch again. According to Val, this was when they'd be wheeling her into surgery.

"Do you think she'll be okay?"

Richard stepped out of their bathroom, a navy bath towel wrapped around his slim hips. "Think who'll be okay?" he asked.

"Val. Today's her surgery." Laura put down her mascara brush and looked at Richard in surprise. How could he have forgotten?

"Oh, sure," he said as he pulled a shirt from a drawer and unfolded it. He walked over to his tie rack and fingered several ties, debating his selection.

"She's probably in surgery right now."

Richard mumbled something and began to dress. As he buttoned his shirt, he asked Laura, "Did I tell you about the new SEC regulations? There was talk about some new ones, but no one knew if it was true. You know how rumors get started." He fastened a cuff and continued, "Well, it turns out that it was true. Stu called me yesterday with a draft of the new legislation. He wants me to review it and give him my comments." Richard finished knotting his tie, pulling the ends with a flourish as he spoke. When Laura did not respond, he said, "That's quite a coup, Laura. I haven't been with the firm that long, and now they're asking for my advice."

"Very nice, Richard." Laura's voice was cool as she made the expected reply. It was, she supposed, good for Richard, and she ought to be glad for him. He'd been so miserable when that job in Chicago had fallen through.

Richard hadn't handled unemployment well, not well at all. That had been one of the worst periods in their marriage. But it was over. Yet even though he was working again, Richard still needed her support. Laura knew that. It was just that today her thoughts were with Val.

She glanced at her watch again, wondering how the surgery was proceeding. Today Val was the one who needed support, and it was obvious that Richard wasn't going to give it.

With a sigh, Laura took one last look in the mirror and went downstairs.

Sid walked through the hospital parking lot, automatically noting the number of cars that bore Knots Landing Motors license plate brackets. That was something he had been adamant about. None of those flimsy dealer stickers that all seemed to go on crooked and peeled off at the first touch of humidity. Sid had insisted that his dealership's advertising be tasteful, finally settling on black brackets with white lettering.

Unfortunately, there weren't all that many Knots Landing Motors license plate brackets to count. Either he wasn't attracting customers from this area, or his customers were all healthy—the latter, he hoped. Sid wouldn't want to make a habit of visiting the hospital, not even if it were good for business.

He scanned the waiting room quickly, searching for the familiar blond head. It wasn't there. The room was nearly empty. An elderly couple sat in one corner, tightly holding each other's hands. The only other occupants were three nurses clustered around a dark-haired man.

Where could Gary be? Sid had been certain he would be here, waiting for the results of Val's surgery. But he wasn't, not unless he had dyed his hair black.

The dark-haired man turned, and Sid understood why the nurses were clustered around him. It was the famous Ewing charm at work. Sid recognized Gary's younger brother Bobby immediately. Bobby had helped Val and Gary move into their house in Knots Landing, and Sid had seen him once or twice since then. Besides, there was something about the Ewing men that made them hard to forget.

"Bobby! What are you doing here?" he asked as he approached the man. The nurses discreetly withdrew, casting glances over their shoulders as they left the room.

"I came to be with Val and Gary." Bobby replied. "Gary called."

Sid could only guess the circumstances of that phone call. If the storm of words had been anything like the damage he had wrought on his bedroom, it was no wonder Bobby was here. Sid wouldn't have been surprised if the entire Southfork contingent had come to lasso in their errant relation.

Sinking into a chair next to Bobby, Sid asked, "Any word on the results of the surgery?"

"Not yet." Bobby shook his head. "It'll be a couple more hours, I think. Gary said something about Val being in the recovery room for a while. I don't think we'll know anything until then."

Sid looked at his watch. It was only midmorning, but somehow it seemed as if it should have been later. Probably because he had already been to the dealership. Karen might laugh and call him a workaholic, but he liked to check on it every morning. Especially since that recent rash of vandalism.

"Where's Gary?" he asked. At first he had thought Gary might have gone out for a walk, but surely he'd be back by now.

"I don't know." Bobby's drawl was more pronounced than usual.

"You don't know?" Had Gary just disappeared? "Have you seen him at all this morning?"

Bobby rose and crossed to the window, the same window where Gary had stood earlier that morning. "Yeah, he was here. He seemed pretty shaky." That was an understatement. "I got the bright idea that

I should try to shock him back to his senses. You know, the old slap-the-hysteric trick. It didn't work." Bobby remembered all too clearly the wounded expression on Gary's face when he left earlier that morning. He hadn't spoken, not even to try to justify himself. He had just walked out, his bowed head and slumped shoulders announcing his defeat.

Sid joined Bobby at the window, his eyes idly counting cars in the parking lot. "He's been pretty shaky since all this started." Sid turned to Bobby. "Did he tell you about the other afternoon?"

Bobby shook his head. "I don't think I want to know. That phone call to our mama was enough."

Sid could understand that. The past few days had been difficult ones for everyone close to Gary Ewing. "As I said, he's been shaky. I can't say that I blame him." Sid's forehead creased and his brown eyes were filled with concern. "Do you have any idea where he went?"

"No, but he seemed about to crumble."

The two men looked at each other, neither willing to voice their primary fear: that Gary had run away again or had turned to alcohol. Each knew Gary well—Bobby as a brother, Sid as a neighbor, employer and friend. Each knew Gary well enough to worry that Val's surgery was more than he could handle.

"I'd better go look for him." There was

a sad tone to Sid's voice, as though he feared what he was going to find.

For a moment Bobby didn't speak. He knew he should go with Sid. After all, Gary was his brother, and Bobby had always had a strong sense of family obligation. But this was one time when Gary was going to have to help himself. He was going to have to take the first step.

"If you find him, tell him I didn't mean what I said," Bobby told Sid.

With a brief nod, Sid headed for the elevators.

He stood outside the front entrance, squinting as his eyes adjusted to the bright sunshine. Shielding his eyes with one hand, he looked around. Where could Gary have gone? Had he taken his car, or gone on foot? Raised in Texas as he was, Gary wasn't one to walk where he could drive. But he might have wanted to stay near the hospital, near Val.

The street in front of the hospital looked less than promising. There were two clinics, an auxiliary parking lot and a veterinarian's office. Desperate as Gary might have been, Sid was certain he wouldn't have gone to any of them.

He walked down the entrance ramp to the street. Right or left? Heads or tails? Without knowing why, Sid turned left and walked to the corner. While he waited for the traffic signal to change, Sid looked down the side alley. At first glance, it appeared no more promising than the street he was following. But as he looked farther, Sid saw the blinking neon sign. That was where Gary was. He was sure of it.

Crossing the street, Sid lengthened his stride. The tacky sign flashed on and off, beckoning the passerby to enter.

The bar's interior was gloomy, and for a moment Sid could barely distinguish the shapes of chairs and tables. Then he saw Gary.

He was seated at the bar, a glass in front of him. Although he was the only patron, the bartender wasn't talking to him. Instead, the man had his back to the bar as he busied himself polishing glasses.

"Gary." Sid took the stool next to his friend, glancing quickly at Gary's glass. Only an inch of the golden liquid remained. *Oh, Gary!* Sid thought, not sure whether to be angry with him or pity him.

Gary looked at his friend, his eyes slow to focus. "Hello, Sid." His voice held a dreamy note Sid had never heard before.

Sid felt pity well in him. Poor Gary! This was what Sid and Karen had feared. Gary hadn't been able to face Valene's surgery; he had taken refuge in alcohol. After the years of abstinence and faithful attendance at A.A. meetings, this wasn't just a shame, it was a crime. Gary Ewing was destroying not just his own life, but his wife's as well.

"Gary, you can't do this." Sid's voice was harsh with anger.

"What'll it be?" The bartender, finally noticing that he had another customer, had ambled over to the bar.

"Nothing." The last thing Sid wanted was a drink. Not here, and certainly not now.

"I'll have another one," Gary said in that same dreamy voice.

"How could you?" Sid reached in front of Gary and snatched the almost empty glass from him. "You and Val have everything. You have each other, a good job, a nice house. You're both young. No matter what happens today, she's going to need you. Good God, Gary, you don't need this."

Gary did not answer.

"Here's your ginger ale," the bartender said, placing a fresh glass in front of Gary.

Sid felt the blood rush to his face. Gary was drinking ginger ale!

"Yeah, it's ginger ale," Gary drawled, seeing Sid's surprised expression. "I had to get out of the hospital. I needed to think, and I couldn't do it there."

Sid had been wrong. Whatever else had happened, Gary hadn't gone off the wagon. Sid's face burned. What kind of friend had he been? He had been quick to assume the worst of Gary. He owed him an apology.

"Gary, I—"

"It's okay." Gary faced his friend, and

his tone was earnest. "I can't blame you for thinking the worst of me. Not when I've been thinking the same things."

"I know this isn't easy—"

Gary shook his head. "Nothing worthwhile ever is."

Sid looked up. Was Gary calling Val's surgery worthwhile? What had happened to change his attitude?

Gary sipped his ginger ale, taking pains to place the glass back on the same water ring. "If Val lives, it's worthwhile. That's all I care about now. Just that she lives, because I can't go on without her." Gary looked at Sid, his blue eyes boring into Sid's brown ones. "That realization is worthwhile, isn't it?"

Sid placed a hand on his friend's shoulder, but he didn't trust himself to speak. This was a new Gary, one he was proud to know.

"I wanted to be ready for anything, but I'm not," Gary confessed. "I'm not ready for Val to die." He paused for a moment, then raised his glass in a silent toast. "But I'm ready for anything else."

Sid lifted the glass he had taken from Gary and touched it to his friend's, a confident smile on his face. Gary was going to be okay.

"The doctors are out of surgery now." One of the nurses gave Gary the news.

Slowly Gary rose from the chair where

he had spent the last two hours. His face was haggard, his lack of sleep evident, but there was a hopeful spring to his step as he followed the nurse to Dr. Harper's office.

The doctor was still in his green surgical outfit and he looked weary, as though the hours in the operating room had drained him both physically and emotionally. Seeing the surgeon's fatigue, Gary felt a moment of panic. Had something unexpected happened to Val? Was that why Dr. Harper looked so tired?

But the doctor's first words dispelled Gary's fears. "I was right!" he said, his voice triumphant. "There's no further evidence of malignancy. And we were able to reconnect the intestine."

Gary stared at the doctor, not taking in what he had heard.

"Your wife didn't have the colostomy," Dr. Harper explained.

Suddenly the reality of his words began to sink in. Val was okay! She would be fine! Tears of relief rose in Gary's eyes. He brushed them aside with the back of his hand, then stood to face the doctor again.

"When can I see her?"

"They'll be bringing her out of recovery soon. You can go to her room to wait."

Gary started for the door, then turned. "Does she know she didn't have the more radical surgery?"

"I told her when she first started to

wake up, but she'll have to be told a few more times before it really sinks in."

Gary flashed a smile of gratitude at the doctor, then hurried toward the elevator. When she was finally brought back to her room, Val was not yet conscious. Her face was pale; her hair was matted from the cap she had worn during surgery; there were tubes and bottles attached to her arms. To an impartial observer, she would have appeared to be a very sick woman. To Gary, she had never been more beautiful.

He pulled the visitor's chair over next to her bed and sat down. For a moment he stared at Val, trying to assure himself that she was real. Then he reached into his shirt pocket and drew out the object he had kept there. Slowly, he slid her wedding ring back onto his wife's limp hand.

"I love you, Val Ewing," he whispered as he bent to kiss her.

Chapter Eight

Beginning Again

"That's one classy car."

Val grinned as she locked the door of her new red convertible. "That's what my husband said." She didn't repeat the rest of Gary's comments—or describe the way they had celebrated the car's arrival. That had all been part of the magical time after she left the hospital. And the happiness had lasted.

Karen had laughed at Val, calling her and Gary honeymooners. But Karen's laughter had been lighthearted, and Val admitted that there was more than a little truth in the accusation. She felt as if her marriage was starting again, that she and Gary had been given a second chance.

For weeks after the surgery, Gary had lunch with Val, something he hadn't done in a long time. Sometimes they would eat at home, sometimes at a restaurant. A few times they packed a lunch and picnicked by the ocean. Through it all, they had been as carefree as teenagers, as happy as newlyweds.

And there was Val's personal victory to delight her, too. She'd enrolled full-time at the local college, and was already knee-deep in reading and writing assignments.

"Valene! Wait up!"

One of Val's new friends caught up with her in the campus parking lot. "I wish I could afford a car like that."

Val smiled at the young man walking next to her. "My husband works for the dealership," she explained. "His discount helped a lot."

Eddie shrugged slightly, readjusting the backpack that held his books. "Are you ready for this class?" he asked. When Val nodded, he continued, "I'm not sure I am. I don't think I want to know what he thought of my story."

Val's face glowed with enthusiasm. "It's the first short story I've ever written. Writing it was hard, but I enjoyed it." She wasn't sure why she had enrolled in creative writing—she had never done anything like that before, and writing wasn't an important part of her life. Why, she never even wrote letters. The phone was much easier and faster. But now that she was in the class, she found it both challenging and fun.

"Maybe you've got a flair for writing," Eddie suggested.

Val could feel the blood rise to her face. Here she was, blushing like a schoolgirl! Well, she *was* a schoolgirl. Just because she was in her thirties didn't change that.

"And maybe I can fly to the moon," she quipped.

But Eddie wasn't fooled by her facetious comment. "I've known you all semester, and I've never seen you this excited."

"To tell you the truth, I do think the story's pretty good," she admitted.

Val and Eddie entered the building and walked down the short corridor to their classroom. It was a modern building, low and sprawling. Some of the classrooms were equipped with electronic blackboards and teleconferencing screens. But the desks were the same ones Val remembered from high school, chairs whose right arm flared into a writing surface.

She slid her books into the wire basket that was attached to the side of the chair and leaned over toward Eddie. "I can't wait to hear what Mr. Leeds has to say about my story. I hope he liked it."

"I heard he's out with the flu this week. We've got some kind of substitute."

Val's expressive eyes mirrored her disappointment. "But we're supposed to get our stories back—"

She broke off suddenly and stared as the instructor entered the room. What was *he* doing here? Val bent her head and stared at her notebook, her thoughts in turmoil. What should she do? Her first reaction was to run out of the class.

"As you may have heard, Professor Leeds is out with the flu, and I will be taking his place." The voice was mellow, cultured and all too familiar. "My name is Earl Trent. I am a writer."

Eddie, who had seen Val stiffen when the instructor walked in, leaned across the aisle toward her. "What is it? Do you know him?"

"Sort of." Her mouth was dry, and she had to force the words out. "My husband knows him."

The instructor continued speaking, his eyes scanning the classroom. "Mr. Leeds gave me your stories to read and asked me to make comments and suggestions." With an arrogant toss of his head, he said, "He seemed to think that because I am one of the few people in southern California who has written something more creative than a license plate, I might have some insights to offer."

There were a few titters as his words registered.

Earl Trent stepped forward a few paces until he reached the first row of chairs. His eyes moved methodically down one row and up the next, as though he were seeking something or someone. When he reached Val, he stopped. Fixing his gaze on her, he waited until she looked up. His dark eyes met hers in a contest of wills.

"I found your stories on the whole sophomoric," he said in a calm voice with an undercurrent of sarcasm. "But as you are sophomores, that can be forgiven." There was a loud gasp as Earl Trent's stiletto-edged words found their mark.

Val shifted in her chair. Earl Trent was singling her out. He recognized her, there was no doubt of that; he knew who she was, and he wanted her to know that. But why? What was he trying to accomplish?

Earl Trent moved back to the professor's desk and picked up a folder. "One story stood out among the rest, so I give you 'The Runaway' by Valene Ewing."

He stood in front of the class, his feet apart, his shoulders squared in a theatrical pose as he began to read.

"'Everybody in my dusty little Tennessee town knew each other from the day they were born. That is why I was so startled to see a stranger, without any shoes on, standing in my mother's kitchen . . .'"

It was a short story, only five pages long, but it seemed to Val that it took Earl an hour to read it. He read in that faintly mocking tone that had marked his speech since he walked in the door, emphasizing the wrong words, making her sweet story seem ludicrous. Val wished she could vanish, disappear into the floor, anything to end this agony.

"'. . . as I closed my eyes in bed that night, that wonderful feeling told me I had made a friend.'" Earl Trent dropped the last page on his desk and turned to the class. "Any comments? Would any of you like to critique this story?"

The students looked at each other. Several of them smiled at Val, offering silent encouragement. Eddie nodded and gave Val the thumbs-up signal.

When none of the students ventured a comment, Earl Trent spoke. "Does the word 'puerile' come to anyone's mind?" he asked. "Aside from the obvious errors of grammar, who can tell me what is wrong with this story?" His voice was haughty, as if to indicate that Val's story was beneath his contempt.

Val suppressed a gasp. She had been so proud of her story, so sure it was good. And now it appeared that she had been wrong. Her story was awful. Her face burned with humiliation.

Eddie raised his hand. "Excuse me, Mr. Trent, but I didn't think it was bad."

Val flashed him a thankful smile.

"You didn't?" Earl raised his eyebrows and gave Eddie a condescending smile. "Well, then, perhaps we need to ask ourselves what elements go into a good story." He looked around the classroom, his eyes cold. "Do you think we might ask of a story that it have believable characters? That it hold our interest? That it express something about the human condition in a novel and interesting way?" He walked back to his desk, picked up Val's story and then tossed it disdainfully onto the desk.

The blood drained from Val's face, and she began to feel light-headed. It wasn't just her story that was being attacked. No, Earl Trent was going beyond her writing, he was attacking her personally. Why? Could it be because of what had happened before? Val's eyes filled with tears.

"I ask you," Earl Trent continued, "should we settle for a namby-pamby rehashing of the most outworn clichés? Idiotic behavior by unbelievable characters? Sentences stuck together like glue?"

She could stand no more. Her face streaming with tears, Val jumped up and ran from the classroom.

The first genuine smile of the morning lit Earl Trent's face. "Was it something I said?" he asked innocently.

Laura crossed her legs and settled back in the deep chair, relaxing for the first time that morning.

"I knew you'd have a suggestion," she said, and a smile crossed her face. "I'm starting to feel comfortable with residentials, but commercial property still bothers me."

Scooter Warren reached for his phone. "Excuse me for a moment while I call the Rolls-Royce dealer and order a Silver Shadow."

"This from the man who said he can't meet the payments on his Mercedes?"

"Well," Scooter drawled, replacing the receiver, "I figured you were going to make me a wealthy man. You're already my top salesperson, and you just told me that you're only *starting* to feel comfortable. If that's true, when you're *really* comfortable, you should be producing double this." He leaned forward and grinned. "I did some quick calculations and decided to take the plunge. Rolls-Royce, here I come."

"You're crazy, Scooter. Did anyone ever tell you that?"

"Unfortunately, yes." He looked at her, his dark brown eyes sparkling with mirth. "Couldn't you at least soften the judgment by saying I'm crazy but lovable?"

Laura uncrossed her legs and began to rise, but Scooter motioned her to remain. "Now that I've solved your problem," he said, "you can help with mine. I've been trying to figure out why you're so much more successful than the other new salespeople."

"I work very hard," Laura said.

Scooter shook his head. "So do they. The difference is, you succeed. You very rarely lose a sale. And I want to know how you do it. Then I can bottle the secret and sell it."

"Essence of Laura Avery?" Laura asked lightly, but she could feel the color rising to her cheeks. While the praise and recognition were welcome, they were also a little overwhelming. She still could hardly believe her own success. It was wonderful, and she loved the heady feeling of making a sale. But it had all happened so quickly that she hadn't really had time to assimilate it. Sometimes it seemed that this was all a dream from which the real Laura, a Knots Landing housewife, Richard's wife and Jason's mother, would soon awaken.

"That's a tough question," she said. "I really don't have an answer."

"I know. I've put you on the spot." Scooter moved around the desk and sat down next to Laura. "It's like the summer the local paper asked me what I had done to become the best shortstop in the league. I couldn't tell them. All I knew was that I played the best I knew how."

"You played ball in college?" Laura was surprised at Scooter's confidence. He had a reputation for keeping his personal and professional lives distinct.

"Actually, this was in high school. I wanted to play football or basketball, but that didn't work out. Who ever heard of a skinny football player or a short basketball star? There weren't too many other choices, so I tried baseball." He smiled, remembering. "I don't know who was more surprised—the coach or me—when I turned out to be good at it."

"I think you'd be good at anything you tried," Laura said. One thing she had learned about Scooter almost as soon as she joined the agency was that he was determined to succeed. There were no roadblocks in Scooter Warren's path, only minor detours.

"Not basketball or football," Scooter said, chuckling.

"But you were good at baseball," she countered.

"Damn good, if I say so myself. In fact, that's how I got my nickname."

"Scooter's not your real name?"

"Come on! Would *you* name a kid Scooter? Even my parents weren't crazy enough to do that."

"But you sign checks that way. I thought it was your real name."

Scooter leaned forward, his expression intent. "This is a cutthroat business, you've seen that. And one of the keys to success is to stand out from the crowd. You do that any way you can. An unusual name is one way. People remember Scooter Warren's name. Do you think they'd remember David Warren or Stephen Warren as clearly?"

"Which one is your real name, Stephen or David?"

"Neither. Scooter is my real name now; I had it changed legally."

"But why Scooter?"

"Oh, my dear, you're making me feel

old. This is all before your time." Scooter laughed, but there was a regretful tone to his voice. "The Scooter was one of the best players on the New York Yankees the year I started to play. I wasn't in his class, then or ever, but he was my idol, and my coach knew it. He started calling me Scooter as a joke. Somehow it stuck, and here I am—a continent and more years away than I want to count—still called Scooter."

The buzzer interrupted Scooter's reminiscences. "Laura has a visitor," the receptionist announced.

"She'll be right out," he replied.

Laura rose to her feet. "Don't forget that you and Mrs. Warren are coming to dinner on Thursday. I'll make a cake shaped like a baseball in your honor."

Scooter put his arm around her shoulders and walked her to the door. "I wouldn't miss it for the world," he said, and there was no mistaking the warmth in his voice.

Karen looked around the office curiously. She had only been there once before, and then only briefly, but she had heard Laura describe it so many times that it seemed familiar.

Karen could see why Laura liked working here. The office was beautifully decorated with traditional furniture and live plants, not the silk trees that so many interior decorators used. The prints on the walls were obviously originals. Everything, down to the color-coordinated telephones, was meticulously planned.

She and Laura had arranged to have lunch together. It was the only time they both had free, and they wanted to start planning Ginger's baby shower.

"Help yourself to coffee. I'd get it for you, but I'm not supposed to leave the phones unattended," the receptionist apologized.

"No problem."

Karen walked in the direction Marge had indicated. The coffee machine was in a small alcove as carefully decorated as the rest of the office. As she waited for the fresh pot of coffee to finish dripping into the carafe, Karen heard a man's voice.

"Scooter in?"

"He is," Marge replied, "but Laura's with him."

"So, what's new?" The man's tone was sarcastic. "Are those two ever out of each other's sight?"

Karen moved restlessly. She didn't like eavesdropping, especially when one of her friends was the subject of the gossip. Would that coffee never finish brewing?

"She's his top salesperson," Marge answered, her voice calm and reasonable.

"If Scooter gave me half the leads he gives her, I'd be top salesman."

"But you don't smile at him." There was an edge to Marge's words, and Karen's discomfort grew. She shouldn't be here, listening to this.

"That's true," the man agreed. "And I'm not writing the book she is."

"Laura's writing a book?" The words were Marge's, but the question was Karen's as well. She hadn't heard anything about Laura writing a book.

"Didn't you hear?" There was no mistaking the bitterness in the man's voice. "It's called *How I Made It Big in Real Estate*. The emphasis is on 'made it.'"

Marge laughed.

I won't listen to any more of this, Karen told herself firmly, and walked back into the office. As she had expected, her appearance halted the gossip. The man walked away from Marge's desk, clearly unwilling to continue the discussion with an audience.

"Maybe I should come back later," Karen suggested.

Marge shook her head. "I'll buzz Laura. She's probably almost done."

Karen took a seat in the reception area and sipped her coffee. She was facing the corner office, and so she saw them as soon as they approached the door. If she hadn't overheard Marge and the other realtor talking, she might have been shocked. As it was, she was still surprised.

Karen had known Laura for a long time, but she had never seen her face so animated, so happy. And the reason wasn't hard to figure out. Scooter had his arm around Laura's shoulders, and his expression could only be described as tender.

I wonder if it's true? Karen asked herself.

"Ready, James?" Gary looked up at the sound of Abby's husky voice. She was standing in the doorway of his office, one hand on her hip, in a pose that, struck by other women, would have seemed contrived, overly dramatic. With Abby, it looked normal. She was, Gary thought, like an exotic bird, turning all other women nearby into drab sparrows.

"James? Who's James?"

She laughed. "Isn't the chauffeur always called James?"

Gary slid the papers he'd been studying into a folder, then filed it away in his drawer. Carefully locking the desk, he rose to his feet. "At your service, *madame.*" He bowed low, doffing an imaginary hat.

"You're terrific. You know that, don't you?" Abby's voice was low and warm.

"All the fair damsels I rescue tell me that."

"Seriously, I do appreciate the ride home."

"And it's such an inconvenience to me!" Gary said with a mock sigh, and laughed.

As they drove home, Abby stretched

her long legs in front of her. "You seem tired."

"I am." The headlights of oncoming cars played across Gary's face, revealing the fatigue he had tried to camouflage at the office. "This streak of vandalism is beginning to worry me."

"Why? The insurance company pays."

"So far." He stopped at a red light and looked over at Abby. "So far it's only cost us the deductible. What I'm afraid of is that the insurance company will cancel our policy."

"Can they do that?"

"Yep."

Traffic was heavier than usual, and for a few moments Gary concentrated on driving.

"Is tonight one of Val's nights out?" Abby asked as she shifted in her seat, crossing one shapely ankle over the other.

"Mmm-hmm. There's not that much time in between her afternoon class and her night class, so she studies at the library." His voice was warm as he thought of his wife. The past few months had been special for both of them.

As though she sensed the direction of Gary's thoughts, Abby's voice held a hint of asperity. "She sure is wrapped up in school."

This time there was no mistaking Gary's enthusiasm. "She loves it. She's like a little kid—except that most little kids hate school, and Val is having the time of her life." *And so am I*, Gary thought. *At least when I'm with her.*

"Why don't you let me cook dinner for you tonight?" Abby kept her voice even. No need to scare him away by seeming too anxious. "Call it payment for the ride home."

Gary glanced over at Abby. He didn't want to insult her—after all, she was just being neighborly. And he had to admit that sometimes it was lonely eating alone. "I don't know. I've got an A.A. meeting tonight. There's barely time for me to grab a sandwich."

Abby chuckled. "Perfect. I'm better at making sandwiches than full-course meals, anyway."

Slowly, hoping not to offend her, Gary said, "I don't think so, Abby. Not tonight. How about a rain check?"

She pouted. "Everybody's always giving me rain checks in a town where it never rains."

Chapter Nine
Sowing Seeds

"You're nervous? Laura Avery the cool and collected, always-in-control Laura Avery is nervous?"

Laura arranged mushrooms in the feed tube of her food processor, careful to keep them aligned so that the slices would be perfect. "I am," she admitted.

"Why?" Karen was seated at the kitchen table, a glass of iced tea in front of her. She had heard the note of panic in Laura's voice when she called to ask Karen to bring over a jar of cardamom. It wasn't at all like Laura to be nervous.

"It's this dinner party. I'm afraid it won't go well."

Again Karen was puzzled. While Laura didn't give dinner parties every week, she was no stranger to entertaining. Why should this particular party be so nerve-racking? "You're a great cook," she said reassuringly. "You'll have Sid and me for moral support. What could go wrong?"

Laura arranged the mushroom slices on a plate, then turned to Karen. "I've never had to entertain the boss's wife before. And I've never met her."

"She'll probably be great. Your boss seems nice."

"Scooter?" Laura smiled. "He's wonderful, and we're a great team. Wait until tonight—you'll see for yourself then."

I bet I will, Karen said to herself. Laura and Scooter had certainly appeared to be a "great team" that day at the office. Out loud, she said, "I can't wait." And it was no less than the truth.

Val stood among the stacks, her head tipped back as she strained to read the call numbers of the books on the top shelf. The bindings were old and the numbers faded, but she persisted. Finally, her eyes narrowed—there it was. Val was so intent on reaching the book she sought, stretching up onto her toes, that she did not see the man quietly duck into the next aisle.

The library was virtually deserted, as it was most evenings at this time. The majority of the day students had gone home for dinner; the evening students had not yet arrived. It was, Val thought, almost like having her own private library.

She returned to her place at one of the small tables, where she sat with two books open in front of her, and a steno pad filled with notes by her right hand. Her brow was furrowed as she compared the two texts. How could they differ so greatly on the same point?

"Burning the midnight oil?"

Val jumped. She hadn't heard anyone approach. As she looked up, her eyes widened with surprise and something akin to fear. What was Earl Trent doing here? Hadn't he humiliated her enough in class? She didn't need any more criticism from him—not here, not now, not ever.

Without waiting for an invitation, Earl took the seat opposite her. "What are you doing here?" he asked, his voice friendly.

I could ask you the same thing, Val thought. Instead, she said nothing.

"Don't you have a husband at home waiting for you?" Earl persisted.

Val's feeling of unease grew. Earl Trent had been deliberately cruel to her in class, leveling a blast of withering sarcasm at her, and now he was trying to be friendly. Why?

Earl raised an eyebrow, obviously waiting for her response.

Perhaps if I answer him, he'll go away, she reasoned. "I have another class later." Her response was cool and clipped, barely civil, but Earl was not discouraged.

"I didn't think anything could come between you and Gary," he said.

What was he suggesting? "Nothing

has," she replied. This time her voice was frigid.

"How've you been? I haven't seen you in quite a while."

The man obviously couldn't take a hint. Well, if he wouldn't leave, she would. The last person on earth she wanted to while away time with was Earl Trent. Val rose from her chair.

Earl rose too. "What's the matter?" he asked softly. "Can't take criticism?"

Val turned and walked away.

But Earl kept pace with her. "If you're going to be a writer, you have to be more thick-skinned than that."

"I never said I wanted to be a writer," she said between clenched teeth. "It was just a story for class."

"But you *should* think about being a writer." His voice was enthusiastic. "You've got talent."

"What?" Val stopped and stared at him. What kind of trick was this? Why would he say she had talent when he had torn her story to shreds, mocking her in front of the class, describing her writing as puerile?

"I was challenging you," Earl explained. "I wanted to see if you could take it."

She said nothing, but her expressive eyes reflected her skepticism.

"I'm sorry. I didn't mean to upset you." He apologized.

Val studied him. How could he say that? His ruthless critique would have upset even a secure, accomplished writer. "If you tear people down like that—"

"I know. I'm sorry." Earl didn't let her finish her sentence. "I've been awful to everyone lately."

He looked contrite, and his words sounded sincere. Part of Val wanted to believe him.

"How's Gary?" he asked.

"He's fine," she replied, her tone guarded.

"Still on the wagon?"

Val flinched. She had never liked that term. "He's still sober," she replied, and the pride she felt in Gary's accomplishment rang in her voice. It had been a difficult time for him, battling alcoholism, but he had won.

"Me, too," Earl told her. "I haven't touched a drop since Judy left me."

"Judy left you?" Val knew that Judy had found it difficult to deal with Earl's drinking. But she was still surprised to learn that they'd separated.

"She went back to New York. I guess that's what she wanted all along." There was a hint of sorrow in Earl's voice, and Val reacted to it instinctively, unable to resist a plea for help.

"I'm sorry," she said.

A bell rang faintly in the distance, and Val looked at her watch. "Time for my class," she said, and began to walk purposefully toward the door.

Earl waved. "Give my regards to Gary."

When the door had closed behind Val, Earl's face broke into a grin, the smile of a man satisfied with himself. *End of Act One*, he told himself.

"Everything's going perfectly," Karen whispered to Laura as they entered the dining room. "See, you didn't have to worry."

Laura looked over the table, taking a last-minute survey. The candles were lit, casting sparkling reflections through the crystal goblets. The flowers, a lovely array of carnations and roses that had been delivered with Scooter's card, were centered on the table. The china and silver were spotless. As Karen had said, everything was perfect.

Even the guests were perfect. Richard, aware of how important this dinner was to Laura, was being unusually affable. Sid and Karen were at their friendliest. And Scooter's wife, Edith, had turned out to be charming. Taller than Scooter by half a head, she was a distinguished woman with silver hair, impeccable grooming and an aristocratic air.

As they entered the dining room, Richard seated Edith Warren on his right, Karen on his left. Karen watched as Scooter seated Laura. Was it her imagination, or did his hands rest on her shoulders a moment longer than necessary? A great team; wasn't that what Laura had called them?

Richard filled Edith Warren's glass from the crystal wine decanter. "I think you'll enjoy this wine. It's a new burgundy, a bit rough and immature but with that eagerness of adolescence. Quite charming in its own way."

"Sounds like my daughter," Edith said drily.

The three couples laughed.

"Isn't your daughter expecting?" Laura asked. "Scooter keeps talking about how he's going to be a grandfather soon."

"That's our older daughter, Sally." A wry smile crossed her face. "Scooter is coming into his own, becoming a grandfather. I'm having a harder time facing being a grandmother."

Karen smiled sympathetically. "I'm having a hard time realizing that my daughter is going to college in a year. I don't know how I'll feel when she has her first child."

"Ambivalent." Edith helped herself to the asparagus. "I'm happy for Sally and excited and yet . . ." There was a wistful tone to Edith's voice.

Sid nodded when Richard offered him more meat. "This veal is wonderful, Laura."

"Laura is the best cook," Karen said, watching her husband load his plate again.

"She's the best everything." Scooter's

voice was warm with admiration. "She's certainly the best salesperson in the office."

A blush rose in Laura's face. Was it the praise? Karen wondered. Lord knew she didn't get much from Richard. Or was it the fact that the praise came from Scooter?

"Incidentally, Laura," Scooter said, leaning toward his hostess, "we've got a nibble on that industrial property on Hill Street. I'd like you to have dinner with the client and me on Tuesday night, and you can work some of your magic."

"Anything you say, boss," Laura answered with alacrity.

Edith Warren was telling a story about her daughter's experiences in college when Scooter asked, "How about your line, Richard? Any hot tips on the market?"

"Richard's an attorney in the investment firm," Laura explained, "not a broker."

"But you must keep your ear to the ground," Scooter persisted.

"Well," Richard admitted, "the investment community is pretty excited about defense industries right now."

Scooter nodded, then returned his interest to Laura. "I hear the Mayberry house is going to be listed again," he said. As the other guests listened to Richard's analysis of the stock market, Scooter continued to discuss real estate with Laura.

A little while later, Richard picked up

the meat platter. "I'll get some more," he said, heading for the kitchen. Edith Warren rose and followed him.

"Once they start talking real estate, it's hard for anyone else to get a word in," she said from the doorway, where she stood watching Richard carve the roast.

"I'm used to shop talk," Richard said. "Laura's accused me of it more than once."

"I suppose so." Edith's words and tone were ambiguous.

"They seem to work well together. Laura's always singing Scooter's praises."

Edith moved to the table and seated herself gracefully, then looked at Richard for a long moment. "I'm sorry," she said at last.

"About what?" Richard continued to arrange slices of veal on the platter. "Shop talk at the table? I've never minded it."

"No." Edith shook her head, her expression sad. "About their being so . . ." She searched for a word. "So obvious."

Richard looked up. What was the woman talking about?

"It'll pass, I'm sure. I guess the worst thing I can do is try to stop them. I'll have to ride it out."

Richard bent his head, pretending to have difficulty cutting a piece of string. What was the woman babbling about?

"You know that Scooter and I are about to become grandparents."

Of course he knew; they had already discussed that. "Yes, I know," he said pleasantly. "Congratulations." *And please get out of my kitchen*, he added silently.

But Edith Warren was not done. "It's a role I feel well suited for. I've been looking forward to it."

That wasn't what she had said a few minutes ago. Richard was beginning to think the woman was rather odd. "That's wonderful," he said, humoring her. "Scooter seems excited, too."

"Yes, he is," she agreed. "But it's taking its toll on him." She rose from the chair and moved to Richard's side. "He's always been such a blatant flirt. His flirting never bothered me, because I knew it never went beyond that. I knew he adored me. But now . . ." Edith sighed. "Such a vital, vigorous man about to be a grandfather. Now he needs more than a flirtation."

Richard's hand froze in midair as the significance of Edith's words hit him. Stunned, he stared at her. "You don't think that he and Laura . . ."

She nodded. "You don't have to protect them."

"Protect them! Why would I protect them? There's nothing going on." How could the woman possibly imagine that Laura would have an affair? Laura wasn't that type of woman.

Edith laid her hand on Richard's arm.

"It's all right, Richard, really. I saw the way you watched them. I knew that was why you came in here."

"I came in here to carve more meat," he insisted.

"Of course." Edith removed her hand from his arm and walked toward the dining room door. "You're being so understanding. I admire that, and I want you to know that I'm taking my cue from you."

The woman's gone off the deep end, Richard thought as she left. And yet . . . what if there were some truth in what she said?

He returned to the dining room with a thoughtful expression on his face.

Sid and Karen were talking to Edith, but it was Laura whom Richard watched. Her face was flushed with animation, and she and Scooter were laughing.

"What's the big joke?" Richard asked, trying to keep his voice calm as doubts assailed him. "Anything we can *all* laugh about?"

Still laughing, Laura answered, "Just real estate talk. You had to be there."

Richard sat down and passed the platter of veal to Karen. As she set it down beside her plate, Scooter rose to his feet.

"I'd like to propose a toast," he said, lifting his glass.

Richard's eyebrows rose.

"A toast," Scooter repeated. "To Laura Avery." He smiled at her warmly. "Who has just broken all previous records by being salesperson of the month for four straight months. And . . ." Scooter paused for effect. ". . . whose commission I now reluctantly have to raise."

They all drank the toast, and then the praise began.

"That's wonderful!" Karen cried.

"Good work, Laura!" Sid congratulated her.

"Wonderful news." Edith's words were friendly, but her voice was cool.

Only Richard remained silent.

"I don't know what to say." Laura's face was lit with excitement. Scooter had never even hinted at an increase in her commission. What a darling he was to announce it tonight, and make her party such a success! "I just don't know what to say," she repeated.

"How about, 'Thanks, I deserve it,'" Scooter suggested. His dark eyes were warm with something more than pride. "You do, you know."

As Laura's eyes met his and she smiled at him, Edith nudged Richard ever so slightly.

"A cocktail, ladies?" The waiter hovered over the table.

"Make mine a glass of milk," Ginger said with a rueful grin. "Junior doesn't take well to alcohol."

"I'll have a diet soda. No caffeine," Val chimed in.

The waiter walked back to the bar, shaking his head. He'd figured them for martini drinkers.

"I'm glad you could meet me," Val said with a smile. "Isn't it funny? We live on the same street, yet we have to meet in a restaurant."

"We certainly don't seem to be keeping the same hours," Ginger said ruefully. "By the time you get home from class, I'm usually asleep." She sipped the milk that the waiter set in front of her. "How is school?"

"If you'd asked me any day but today, I'd have said wonderful. Today, I don't know." And Val recounted her experience in Earl Trent's creative writing class.

"The man ought to be boiled in oil!" Ginger exclaimed.

"My sentiments exactly. Unfortunately, I think the California penal code frowns on things like that."

"How about voodoo?"

"Sounds wonderful to me, as long as it works. But what about you, Ginger? How are you doing? What are you learning in Lamaze?"

Ginger laughed, then began to rub her stomach. "It looks silly, and it feels even sillier when you're doing it, but everyone who's been through the class swears that it's the greatest thing."

"That's what Karen told me." Val remembered the day she had first helped

Ginger with her exercises—the same day that Dr. Harper had called with the frightening news. It seemed part of another lifetime, but it had been only a few months ago.

"How's Kenny doing in Lamaze?"

"Okay." Ginger's voice suddenly sounded reserved, and Val realized she did not want to discuss her husband. With a sigh, Val picked up her soda.

Laura wiped the cleanser from her face with the tissue, took a final look in the mirror, and sat on the side of the bed. "You were very nice to Scooter and Edith tonight," she said. "I appreciate it."

"Why shouldn't I be nice?" Richard finished toweling his hair dry, then walked to his side of the bed. He had one thing on his mind, and it wasn't Scooter Warren. He slid between the sheets, turned out the light and reached for his wife.

"Scooter's very important to me," Laura said, and Richard could hear the warmth in her voice. "I felt you were supporting me tonight, and I liked it."

She kissed Richard lightly, then turned on her side.

"I was very proud of you, too," Richard murmured, pressing kisses on the back of Laura's neck. A hint of her perfume lingered, tantalizing him. There was no one like Laura. He whispered her name and began to massage the back of her neck.

"G'night, Richard," she murmured, her voice thick with sleep.

Tense with frustration, Richard rolled back to his side of the bed. Was Edith right? He gritted his teeth. She couldn't be right!

A smile crossed Gary's face as he watched Val reach for her cleansing cream. "Okay, let's have it," he said.

"Let's have what?" Val turned to look at him in the mirror.

"Whatever it is that's on your mind. You've brushed your hair for five minutes straight, and now you're cleaning your face for the second time. You're a thousand miles away. Did something happen at school, or was it seeing Ginger?"

Val wrinkled her nose. "I got my story back in my writing class."

"So? Did Mr. Leeds like it?"

This time Val turned and faced Gary directly. "He had the flu. We had a substitute."

"And . . . ?" Gary prompted her.

"It was Earl Trent."

Gary considered Val's statement in silence. What was it about Earl Trent's reappearance that bothered Val so much?

"He really tore into my story. He read it to the class and made me feel like an idiot."

Gary clenched his fists. That sounded exactly like the kind of cowardly thing

Earl Trent would do, take advantage of a position of power to belittle someone. "So stay away until Leeds gets back," he suggested. *And keep Trent out of our lives*, he added silently.

"Do you think I should?" Val climbed into bed and put her arms around Gary, drawing comfort from his nearness.

Gary nodded. "Did he say anything else?"

Val's arms tightened almost imperceptibly, but Gary was aware of her tension. Damn Earl Trent! Hadn't he caused enough trouble?

"After class I saw him in the library. He tried to be nice, but . . ." Val paused, trying to verbalize her fears. "I could hardly talk to him. He made me feel so . . . uneasy."

Gary turned to hold Val in his arms. "You don't owe that man anything. Just stay out of his way."

"I will," she promised.

Val forced herself to relax. It was okay. That awful feeling of dread was just nerves, sheer imagination. "Judy left him. Did you know?"

"No."

Long after Val had fallen asleep, Gary lay awake. So Judy had left Earl. How was Earl dealing with that? If he was the same Earl, not well, Gary guessed. Not well at all.

Chapter Ten
Growing Doubts

"Creamed turkey on toast. I wonder if it tastes as awful as it looks."

Val laughed. "My classmates say it does. If I were you, I'd stick to something simple like a sandwich." Following her own advice, Val selected a plate labeled "Ham and Swiss on Rye" and placed it on her tray.

Karen eyed the sandwiches suspiciously, then settled for a cottage cheese and fruit platter. "You know," she said as they found an empty table, "it's weird being almost the only person over thirty."

"I know. Sometimes I feel like an old lady." Val grinned. "But most of the time I forget, and I just enjoy the classes. I can't believe how much fun I'm having here."

Karen smiled. It was good to see Val so happy. She had worried that Val would become more cautious, less exuberant, as a result of her recent scare, but she had bounced back and seemed to be enjoying life more than ever before. And Gary seemed like a new man.

"I wonder if Diana would like it here," Karen speculated.

Val shrugged. "If it means anything, I love it. I'll be glad to tell her all about it."

"I have a feeling she wants to go out of town." There was a faint sadness in Karen's dark eyes. "I suppose it's that empty nest syndrome we've all read about, but sometimes I can hardly believe she's so grown up; I miss the little girl she used to be."

"I know." Val thought of her own daughter. Lucy was a teenager now, and Val had missed the joy of watching her grow up. She brushed those thoughts aside, knowing that they would bring only unhappiness. She had to focus on today, on the good things in her life.

"Now, what are we going to do for Ginger's shower?" she asked. "Where shall we have it?"

"What do you think about having it at a restaurant? Then none of us will have to fuss with decorating and cleaning up."

Val wrinkled her nose. "If it's going to be a surprise, I think it would be easier to have it at one of our houses." She took a swallow of her soda, then offered, "I'll be glad to have it at my house. You know I love to throw parties."

"Are you sure? With school and every-thing, isn't that too much work?"

Val grinned and shook her head. "Really, I'd like to. Now, who should we invite? Laura, of course, and Abby. Who else?"

Before Karen could reply, a male voice broke into their conversation. "May I join you?"

Val's face registered her surprise as she looked up. "Oh, hi, Earl."

He stood there, a stupid smile on his face, waiting. Pulling over a chair from the next table, he sat next to Val. "I picked these up for you," he said as he handed her two books. "They're short stories by two southern writers I thought you should read."

Val glanced at the titles on the spines. The nervous way she handled the books told Karen that she was uncomfortable with this man, that she didn't know how to react.

"Both of these authors use the southern idiom in a manner similar to yours," Earl said, his eyes intent on Val's face. "You can learn from their structure."

Val nodded but said nothing. Karen's dark eyes moved from her friend to the stranger; the undercurrents of tension between the two of them were tangible.

"You do have talent," Earl continued, his eyes meeting Val's and holding them. "You have a voice of your own that you need to cultivate."

And still Val did not respond. Karen was reminded of the tales she had heard of people being mesmerized by the slow movement of a snake about to strike. Val had that look, but if Karen had anything to say about it, Val was not going to be this snake's victim.

"I love the way Val talks," Karen said, deliberately twisting Earl's meaning. "She's got so many expressions that are—"

"Carson McCullers is another writer you might want to read," Earl continued, as though Karen weren't there. "Your writing reminds me of her."

"Do you really think I can write?" Val said in a low voice, her words hesitant, as though she feared the answer.

"No—"

Val's blue eyes flew open in shock, and Karen flinched. How could the man be so cruel?

"Not yet." As Earl finished the sentence, the color returned to Val's face. "You begin your stories at the beginning. A good story begins in the middle, recalls the beginning, then proceeds to the end."

Her face mirroring her confusion, Val said, "That sounds crazy."

"I know, but it works." Earl's voice was low and mellow, and he spoke as though Val were the only person in the room. "Maybe we can get together sometime. I can go over your story with you to show you what I mean." His voice deepened, becoming almost seductive. "You've got talent, but it's got to be developed. I want to help you."

His last words were said in an almost pleading tone, and Karen watched the play of emotions on Val's expressive face. She seemed to distrust the man, yet she wanted to believe his words.

"It's the least I can do after the way I treated you."

"How did you treat her?" Karen asked, trying once more to break the spell this man was weaving.

This time Earl acknowledged her existence. "Rough. I guess I've watched too much TV—you know, the crusty professor being tough on the most promising students." He rose and pushed his chair back to the other table. "It works on TV." Giving Val an odd smile, the man walked away.

"Well, he certainly seems to think a lot of you," Karen said, studying Val's face.

Val was silent for a moment. Then she explained, "Gary and I knew him before he came to teach here."

So that was why he used such a familiar tone with Val. He wasn't just a professor. Karen began to relax.

"He's the husband of—" Val broke off and started her sentence again. "He was married to the woman I told you about."

"What woman?"

Val looked down at her tray, unwilling

to meet her friend's gaze. "Judy Trent."

"Judy? The one Gary . . . ?" For a moment, Karen was transported back in time to the morning when Val had learned that Gary had lied to her, that Judy was much more than just the wife of a fellow alcoholic. With tears streaming down her face, Val had begged Karen to tell her what to do. Gary and Val had managed to face up to their problems and rebuild their marriage, and Karen had thought that the painful incident was part of the past, over and forgotten as much as it ever could be. But now she wasn't so sure. This man's reappearance made her nervous.

"Does he know about it?" she asked. "Earl—does he know about Judy and Gary?"

Still looking at her plate, Val shook her head. "I don't think so. At least, he hasn't mentioned it." She raised her eyes to Karen's. "He seems so sad."

Karen's feeling of dread increased. If there was anything Val couldn't resist, it was someone who needed her.

The office was empty when Richard opened the door. Laura's jacket was hung over her chair, but there was no other sign of her. She had to be there. If she had been out with a customer, she would have worn her jacket. Where was she? A prickle of unease ran down his neck.

He glanced around the office, then saw

the light from behind a partially closed
door in the corner. It was Scooter's office;
perhaps Laura was there working with
him. Richard walked toward the corner
office.

"We've had some good times, too,
haven't we, kid?" Scooter's voice carried
into the main room.

Richard heard the murmur of Laura's
reply but could not distinguish her words.

"And it's just beginning," Scooter said.
There was no mistaking the affection in
his voice, a tone that caused Richard to
move more quickly.

As he stepped into Scooter's office,
Richard recoiled instinctively. His wife
was perched on the corner of Scooter's
desk, and Scooter had his arm around
her, his lips only millimeters from her
face. As though watching it in instant
replay, Richard saw Edith Warren's face as
she had said, "Now he needs more than a
flirtation." At the time he had dismissed
her innuendos. But now?

"Richard!" Laura's voice sounded more
high-pitched than usual.

Scooter dropped his arm and moved
away from Laura, holding his hand out to
greet Richard.

Richard ignored the outstretched hand.
"I was supposed to pick you up tonight,"
he said, his eyes never moving from his
wife's face. "We're going to dinner,
remember?"

"Of course I remember." Laura slid down from the desk and straightened her skirt. "I've been expecting you."

Richard didn't even try to hide the sarcasm in his voice. "You'd never know it."

"I'll be just a minute," Laura excused herself.

There was a moment's silence. Then Richard said, "I hope I didn't interrupt anything."

"Interrupt?" Scooter's voice was innocent. "No, we were just going over some listings."

"Is that what they call it these days?" Richard used the stinging voice that used to intimidate witnesses, but it had no effect on Scooter.

"Ready," Laura said as she re-entered the office.

"Are you sure? Maybe you have some more 'work' to do." Richard's lips twisted as he pronounced the word.

"Don't be silly." Laura took her husband's arm and led him toward the door. "Come on."

At the door, Richard glanced over his shoulder. Scooter was watching them, a thoughtful expression on his face.

"You know, Gary, I really do appreciate your driving me home." As Abby fastened her shoulder harness, she leaned more to the left than absolutely necessary, and her arm brushed Gary's.

He smiled absentmindedly, then put the car in gear.

"Worried again?" she asked, her voice low and intimate.

Gary nodded as he pulled out into traffic. "It's that vandalism."

"Maybe I can help you." She put a hand on Gary's arm, her long fingers tightening ever so slightly. "You know I'm worried about the dealership, too." Her violet eyes radiated sincerity.

They drove in silence for a few moments. Then Abby asked, "Does Val have a class tonight?"

"Nope." Gary shook his head. "Just an afternoon class. She's probably home now. Why?"

"Just wondered." Abby shifted closer to him. "Next time Val has a night class, you and I ought to plan something."

Gary glanced over at her. "Like what?"

Abby shrugged. "A hamburger . . . a salad . . . something like that." There was a plaintive note in her voice as she explained, "I do miss the company of adults."

He shifted uncomfortably. Hadn't they had this discussion before? He thought he had resolved the situation then. "I've got my A.A. meetings," he said.

"You could miss one now and then, couldn't you?" Abby's hand tightened possessively on his arm.

"I try not to." Her perfume filled his

nostrils, but tonight it seemed cloying rather than seductive. Gary moved his arm, trying to make it look accidental but hoping Abby would remove her hand.

"Am I making you nervous?" There was a hint of amusement in her low voice.

Damn right! Gary thought. *This conversation is heading in a direction I don't like.* He responded to her question with one of his own. "Why should you make me nervous?"

"I don't know. That's why I asked. It's just that every time I suggest spending a little time together, you seem to get flustered."

"If I do, it's news to me." His reply was sheer bravado. Abby *did* make him nervous. He wasn't sure what she was up to, and that worried him. Gary Ewing liked to know where he stood with people.

"Is it because you're a man and I'm a woman?" she persisted.

Gary shrugged again. "Could be."

"Now, think about it. Isn't that silly?" Abby's voice was persuasive. "We're neighbors. We work together. We like each other. Why shouldn't we spend a little time enjoying each other's company?"

She made it sound so innocent, but one thing Gary knew about Abby Cunningham was that she was far from innocent.

"It's because I'm a woman and you're a man. Right?" she asked again.

There was a touch of anger in Gary's voice as he responded to her goading. "You make it sound like that shouldn't make any difference."

"Does it have to?" Abby stretched her arm along the seat back, smiling in the darkness as Gary flinched when her fingers touched the back of his neck. Why wouldn't he admit that he found her attractive? She wasn't used to having men resist her.

"Maybe it doesn't have to make a difference," he said, "but it could."

"Even if it did . . . even if something did happen . . . it wouldn't be the end of the world, would it?"

Gary's only response was to press the accelerator closer to the floor.

"Men say that to me all the time. 'It wouldn't be the end of the world. We could keep it in perspective,' they say." She paused, then continued so softly that Gary could barely hear her words, "They could be right."

Three more blocks and we'll be home, Gary told himself. *Three more blocks.*

Abby watched his discomfort for a few seconds, then laughed lightly. "Just kidding, Gary," she said, and touched his hand in a fleeting caress. "Just kidding."

As he pulled into the cul-de-sac, Gary forced himself to laugh, but it was a laugh of relief that they were home. He had no doubt what Abby wanted. But why him?

* * *

"It's that overactive imagination of yours, Karen," Sid said, handing her the dinner plates.

Karen continued loading the dishwasher. "I was right about Richard and Abby, wasn't I?"

"Yes," Sid answered reluctantly. He hadn't wanted to believe Karen when she warned him that his sister was having an affair with Richard. But Karen had been right. Was she right again?

"I just have a feeling Laura's giving Richard a dose of the same medicine."

He poured himself another cup of coffee and sat at the table. "You sound happy about it. When it was Richard and Abby, you thought it was terrible."

"I know, but Richard's treated Laura pretty badly. If she's finally found someone who appreciates her, I think she deserves him."

Sid stared at his wife, surprised. "I've heard about double standards, but this takes the cake."

"It's not a double standard," Karen protested. "It's a single standard."

"But when it was Abby—"

The sound of water filling the dishwasher drowned out the end of Sid's sentence. As Karen sat down at the table, she asked, "Did I tell you about the man who's teaching Val's writing class?"

* * *

"Ooh, that's wonderful," Val sighed as Gary rained kisses down the side of her neck, touching the sensitive hollows of her collarbone. "Don't stop."

"I wasn't planning to," he murmured between kisses.

Val laid her hands on both sides of his face and drew his lips down to hers. "I love you," she whispered before her lips parted beneath his.

"I love you, too, sweetheart."

The shrill ringing of the phone abruptly interrupted them.

"Don't answer it," Gary whispered.

She reached for the phone. "It could be important—maybe Lucy, or an A.A. call."

"They'll call back."

But Val lifted the receiver to her ear. "Hello?" She sat up as the caller identified himself. "Earl, what is it?"

"What the hell does *he* want?" Gary demanded, turning on the light.

Val shushed her husband. "Now, don't drink, whatever you do," she said into the phone. "We'll be right there."

"What?" There was no mistaking the annoyance in Gary's voice.

"You're going to be okay until we get there." Val kept her voice positive. "You won't take a drink."

She hung up the phone and swung her legs out of bed. "He says he's going to take a drink."

"Let him."

Val turned to her husband in surprise. "Gary!" This wasn't like him. Gary knew how difficult abstinence was; he had fought the battle every day for so long. It wasn't like him to give up on another alcoholic, even Earl Trent.

"Val, he's using you."

"No, he's not. Earl's in trouble and he needs someone." Her voice was filled with concern.

"He just wants someone to hold his hand." Gary remembered how many times Earl had gotten drunk merely to arouse Judy's compassion. Now he was pulling the same trick with Val, and Gary didn't like it one bit.

"Holding hands is what we're here for. Come on, Gary, get dressed." Val grabbed a pair of jeans and a shirt from her closet.

"Don't you see, Val?" Gary sat on the edge of the bed and faced her. "I don't know whether or not Earl knows . . . about Judy and me, I mean." He said the words reluctantly. It was a part of his life he was ashamed of, and he hated even talking about it. "If he does, seeing me might make him start to drink again."

Val looked at him steadily for a moment. "All right then; I'll go alone."

"No!" Gary was adamant. He was not going to leave his wife alone with Earl Trent.

"What choice do I have?"

"Neither of us has to go."

Val pulled a pair of shoes from the closet. "If neither of us goes, he'll drink."

"That's his problem." Gary's voice was cold.

"No, it's not." She slid her feet into the shoes. "It's *our* problem. You *can't* let that man down again—or can you?"

Gary's eyes met hers, but he said nothing.

With a toss of her blond hair, Val turned and ran down the stairs.

Earl was seated at the bar, a glass of amber liquid in front of him, when Val slid onto the stool next to his.

"I don't know," he said, picking up the drink and staring at it as though mesmerized. "I don't know if I can make it."

"Earl, you *can* make it." Val poured every ounce of conviction she possessed into those words. She had to stop him before he took that first drink.

Earl lifted the glass closer to his mouth.

The bar door swung open, and the sound of rapid footsteps behind her made Val turn. "Gary!" She hadn't expected him to come.

Gary focused his attention on the man next to Val. "What do you think you're doing?"

"He hasn't taken a drink, Gary," Val told him.

"No," Earl said, smiling slyly at Gary, "I've been waiting for you to come and save me, just like you did so many times before."

Gary's lip curled in disgust. "I'm not going to play games with you. You want to drink, drink. Just don't ask Val and me to watch you."

He took his wife's hand and pulled her toward him, and she slid off the stool. Together they took a step toward the door.

"You were supposed to be my friend. What happened to you, Gary?" Earl's voice was plaintive.

Gary turned and faced the man at the bar. "I got sick of being used. You didn't want a friend; you wanted a nursemaid."

Earl's face was contorted with pain. "You said you'd always be there. Then one day you weren't. You both left at the same time, you and my wife."

Gary put his arm protectively around Val's shoulders. God! He wished she didn't have to listen to this.

"I don't know about Judy, but I got sick of talking you into being sober. You want to be sober? Don't drink. You want to drink? Be my guest."

"Gary!" Val was shocked. What was it about Earl Trent that brought out this cruel streak in Gary?

"We're not doing him a favor by playing these games."

As Gary and Val walked out the door, Earl stared after them. This wasn't working the way he had planned.

Chapter Eleven
Bitter Harvest

Karen's eyes widened in surprise as she glanced out the window. It was nine-thirty, and Laura's car was still in the driveway. Punctual Laura who always left the house at exactly eight forty-seven was still home. With a worried frown on her face, Karen walked over to the Averys' house.

"There you are." There was a hint of relief in her voice when she discovered Laura, dressed for work except for her suit jacket, seated on her patio drinking coffee. "Aren't you going to work?"

Laura smiled a welcome. "My first appointment isn't until eleven, so I thought I'd take it easy this morning."

"Sounds like a good idea. I guess your boss wouldn't mind."

"He won't." The smile in Laura's voice made Karen look up sharply.

"Your boss sure is cute," Karen said as she poured herself a cup of coffee from the carafe on the patio table.

"Isn't he?" Again there was that affection in Laura's voice.

"It must be nice working for him."

"It is. As I told you, we're a great team." Laura smiled, remembering how helpful Scooter always was, and how he had surprised her by raising her commission. Yes, it was fun working for Scooter Warren.

"Is he as nice to you as he seems to be?"

Laura's eyes narrowed slightly. Karen certainly was inquisitive this morning. No one had ever accused her of being reticent; if Karen wanted to know something, she asked. But this was more heavy-handed than usual.

"Karen, are you hinting at something?" Laura asked bluntly.

"Who, me?" Karen's eyes widened innocently. "No. Are you?"

"Am I what?" Laura was confused. This conversation was getting stranger by the minute. She had the feeling she was part of a play, but no one had given her a script.

"Are you trying to tell me something?" Karen persisted.

At least that was easy to answer. "No."

"So you're not saying anything?"

Now Laura had the feeling she was

being cross-examined. It ought to be Richard doing the questioning—that was his forte, not Karen's.

"About what?"

"About you and . . . oh, never mind." Karen sipped her coffee and looked intently at her neighbor. It wasn't like Laura to be so evasive. Perhaps Karen's suspicions were well-founded after all.

"Ms. Ewing, could you stay for a moment?" Earl's voice was properly professorial as he called to Val at the end of class. She approached his desk, a question in her blue eyes, and he gestured for her to sit down in the front row.

Earl waited until the classroom was empty, then took the seat next to her.

"I made an ass of myself last night," he said. Now his voice was anything but professorial.

Val wished he wouldn't talk about last night. The scene in the bar was one she didn't care to relive. "You didn't take that drink, did you?"

"No."

"That's all that matters."

"I guess . . ." Earl looked out the window, as though trying to marshal his thoughts. "Val, why did Gary quit on me the way he did?"

The question took her by surprise. "Quit on you? How?"

He faced her again, his eyes probing.

"For a while he was like a guardian angel."

Val smiled faintly, trying to visualize her husband as an angel. That was hardly a word she would normally use to describe him.

"Not a cherub, more like a warrior." Earl had seen her smile and answered it. "Every time I got near a drink, he'd storm in, calling me every name in the book, and drag me out of bars, anything to keep me from drinking. Sometimes I hated him for it, and sometimes I loved him."

Val nodded, listening as Earl poured out his emotions. "Then he stopped. One night he didn't come." Earl's voice deepened, and Val had the fleeting thought that he was reciting lines he had rehearsed. Ridiculous! No one practiced a speech like this.

"Maybe Gary figured it was time for you to do it on your own," she suggested.

"I don't think so. I wasn't really drinking. I was just threatening to so he'd come and drag me home."

Val remembered Gary's comment that Earl used people, that he wanted a nursemaid.

"Maybe he just thought it was pointless."

Earl stood up and wandered to the window. "First he stopped coming after me, and then Judy left. Almost as if there were a connection." He turned and walked back to Val. "Was there a connection?"

Val looked at the floor, not wanting to face Earl. This was what Gary had been afraid of, that Earl would find out about him and Judy, that he would fall apart, start drinking again. Oh, why couldn't the past disappear?

"You don't want to tell me about it, do you?" Earl's voice reflected his hurt. "You're afraid it will send me off the deep end." He sat next to Val again and took her hand. "You don't have to worry about me. I can handle it. I just wondered if you knew about it."

Val steeled herself not to pull her hand away, even though Earl's grip was painful. A.A. had taught her how important physical contact was when people were fighting deep emotional problems, that the grip of a hand could be the lifeline a person needed.

"I knew." Her voice was almost inaudible. This was awful!

As though he sensed her embarrassment, Earl said. "Well, don't you feel better now that we've gotten that out in the open? Now we can get back to the business of literature."

He rose and went to his desk, coming back with a manila folder. "I have some ideas about how you could improve your story." Once again his voice was professorial. "With a little work, I think it could be good enough to submit to the college literary magazine."

"Really?" Val was having trouble adjusting to Earl's mercurial change of mood.

"I mean it. It just needs a little . . ." Earl gestured with his hands. "Let's face it; we need to take it all apart and find a way to put it back together. Suppose I come over tonight and—no, I don't suppose Gary would like that." He paused. "You could come over to my house."

This was all happening so quickly. One minute they were talking about Gary and Judy, and now Earl wanted to work on her story. Val needed time to think. "I don't know," she said.

"It'll just take an hour or two. Come at eight and you'll be home by ten." He ripped a piece of paper from a notebook and scribbled on it. "Don't say no, Val. Here's my address. I'll see you tonight."

Without giving her a chance to reply, Earl left the room. As he strode down the hall, he was smiling broadly. Act Two was over.

Laura was fastening her earrings when Richard entered the bedroom.

"You smell wonderful," he said as he bent to kiss her. "And that dress is great. I'll be the envy of every man tonight."

"Tonight?" Laura looked at him blankly.

"Dinner at an intimate French restaurant, a late-night drive to the ocean, and then . . ." Richard ran his hand down her arm, caressing it suggestively.

"I can't." Laura touched her hair, making certain the pins were secure. "Tonight Scooter and I are having dinner with a client. Can't we do it tomorrow?"

"Laura, do you have any idea how hard it is to get reservations at Chez Nous? I practically had to beg them on bended knee and promise our firstborn son if we were ten minutes late."

"Honey, I'm sorry. I thought you heard Scooter and me talking about it the other night."

Scooter! If he heard that man's name one more time, Richard thought grimly, he'd wring someone's neck. "I guess I wasn't hanging on his every word the way you were," he said, not bothering to hide his anger.

"Can't we do it another time?" Laura's tone was cajoling, but Richard was in no mood for persuasion.

"You spend more time with Scooter than you do with me and Jason," he said, his voice rising sharply. "Oh, but of course, we can't advance your career."

"Richard!" Laura rose and faced him. What had gotten into him?

"I don't like this master-slave relationship you've got with Scooter."

Laura's anger, generally slow to start, began to simmer. "You're describing the way *our* relationship used to be. You're just upset that it isn't like that anymore."

Once she had stayed home, content to be Richard's wife and the mother of his son. Going to work hadn't been her idea; she had done it because they needed the money. But now she enjoyed the responsibility and the sense of independence it gave her. It was Richard who was having trouble coping with their changed relationship.

"So you've found some other man to be a geisha to."

Laura clenched her fists, willing herself not to shout at Richard. That last comment had been too much. Maybe innuendos worked well in a courtroom, but she didn't appreciate them in her home.

"You don't think I can succeed on my own, do you?" she demanded. "If I'm doing well in my work, the only reason you can figure is that I'm sleeping with the boss."

"That's not what I'm saying."

"It's exactly what you're saying." Laura's voice was low and controlled; only the tense muscles of her jaw betrayed her anger. She stared at him for a moment, still unable to believe his veiled accusations. "Some men and women can like each other without going to bed together. Just because you can't do it doesn't mean everyone can't. Richard, we're not talking about you and Abby; we're talking about me and Scooter, and it's an entirely different story."

Picking up her evening bag, Laura walked calmly and deliberately out of the house. She would not give Richard the satisfaction of seeing how his suspicions had wounded her. It was only when she was in her car that she gave vent to her emotions.

Damn the man! Why did he have to spoil her evening? She pounded her fists angrily on the steering wheel.

"'I never saw the stranger again after that day. He disappeared as mysteriously as he had come.'" Val looked up from the sheet of paper, perplexed. "But that isn't what happened, Earl. He became a friend of our family, and I saw him all the time."

Earl, who had been wandering about the room while she read, walked back from the door, sliding something into his pocket. "That's what we need to work on, the difference between fiction and reality. That's what your writing needs, an appreciation of the distinction between life and literature."

He sat down next to her and began to point out the changes he had made in her story.

Two hours later, Val closed the folder. "Well, if that's everything, I guess I'll be going."

Earl put a restraining hand on her arm. "We've got lots more to talk about."

Val glanced at the clock. "I told Gary I'd

be back by ten," she said, remembering her husband's angry reaction when she had told him she was going to Earl Trent's house. Gary had insisted that Earl was feeding her a line, luring her to his house under the pretense of helping her polish her story. But Gary had been wrong. Earl *had* helped her with her story. He had shown her how to heighten the suspense, how to make the action more dramatic and the characters more believable. It had been a working evening, pure business. Why, then, was she starting to feel uneasy?

"Let Gary worry," Earl said. "It will be good for him."

"I don't think so." The twinges of uneasiness began to intensify.

Earl moved nearer to Val. "Are you afraid of me?" he asked, his face only inches from hers.

"Of course not," she lied.

Earl put his arm around her shoulders and drew her closer. "Maybe you should be," he said.

The restaurant was one of the most exclusive in the Los Angeles area, a Victorian mansion that had been turned into an elegant and intimate dining spot. The rooms were small and the tables widely spaced, giving patrons the illusion that they had their own private mansion. When Laura arrived, Scooter was waiting for her.

"I thought Chuck Lapin was coming," she said when the waiter had seated them at a table for two.

Scooter shook his head. "He canceled at the last minute, but reservations here are so hard to come by that I didn't want to waste them."

And so they ate alone, discussing various clients and properties. It was only when the waiter had brought them their after-dinner drinks that Scooter leaned forward.

"Laura, what's bothering you? You've been looking at me strangely all evening." The lines around his eyes deepened as he frowned slightly .

Laura flushed. All night she had been recalling Richard's accusations and the strange conversation she'd had with Karen that morning, despite her efforts to ignore them, to concentrate on the things Scooter was saying. And Scooter, it seemed, was aware of her preoccupation.

"Oh, it's nothing."

Scooter shook his head, obviously not believing her. It was all so silly. How could she tell him what Richard and Karen had thought?

"Anything you want to talk about?" He put his hand over hers and pressed it lightly, as though reassuring her.

The touch of his hand reminded Laura of the times she had confided in Scooter, the times he had understood when no one else could. Suddenly she was sure that he would understand this time, too, and he'd laugh with her. Together they'd banish the ugly rumors.

Raising her eyes to his, Laura asked, "Do you realize everyone assumes we're having an affair?"

For a moment, Scooter said nothing. *He's as shocked as I was,* Laura thought. But his reply surprised her.

"To tell the truth, I had heard the rumors." He smiled a little self-consciously. "I didn't want to squash them, because they made me look so good."

He paused, and Laura laughed because she knew he expected it. But, damn it, it wasn't funny.

"I guess rumors are inevitable when a man and a woman work together," Scooter said. "You can't take them seriously."

She toyed with her earring nervously. "But why does it have to be inevitable?" she asked. "If you had a male business associate, nobody would say a word if you went out to dinner together or spent time with each other. Everyone would know it was business."

He shrugged, obviously not as concerned as Laura. "I guess a lot of people haven't caught up with the times."

The waiter brought their drinks, and Laura sipped hers before she spoke again.

"I like being with you because we work well together. Sleeping with you never crossed my mind."

A slow flush rose in Scooter's face. "Never?" he asked.

To cover her confusion, Laura raised her glass and took another sip. "Well, I don't mean it never crossed my mind, but I didn't seriously consider it."

He smiled, and his brown eyes were warm again. "I'd hate to think that you hadn't even thought about it."

"Have you?"

Scooter chuckled. "Laura, you're a very beautiful woman. Any man with a normal supply of hormones would think about having an affair with you. But," he added slowly, "there's a difference between thinking and doing."

Laura reached across the table and squeezed his hand. This was the Scooter she knew, the man who understood her. "You know why I wouldn't have an affair with you, don't you?" she asked.

"Tell me."

"Because I like you too much." Laura raised her eyes to his. It was so important that he understand! "We're both married. You have a good marriage. Mine? Well, Richard and I have problems, but we're working on them."

He nodded.

"If you and I had an affair, we'd be risking two marriages," she continued. "We might get to the point where in order to save those marriages, we'd have to give each other up." She tightened her grip on Scooter's hand. "I'd hate that!"

"So would I." There was a hint of sadness in his voice, but he managed a smile.

She smiled back. "I guess it's better to keep on being friends than to be more than friends and wind up with nothing at all."

For a moment, Scooter said nothing. Then he raised Laura's hand to his lips and pressed a kiss on it.

"You're one hell of a friend," he said.

"Is the thought of me as a lover so ridiculous?"

The color drained from Val's face as she stared at him. Earl? A lover?

"Why not?" he continued, smiling slightly at her discomfiture. "Because you're married? Gary was married. That didn't stop him." He stared at Val for a long moment, then asked, "Don't you want to get even with him?"

"No!" Get even with Gary? Why would she want to do that? All she wanted was to let the past remain in the past.

She started to rise, but Earl pressed her back on the couch. "I want to get even with Gary," he announced, "and you're the only way I can."

Suddenly all of Val's misgivings, those vague feelings of dread that she had dismissed, crystalized. Gary was right—Earl had been using her. He had planned this from the very beginning, from the moment he discovered she would be in his class. A sick feeling settled in her stomach.

She scrambled up, pushing at Earl as he tried to prevent her. "You can't do this," she said, backing away toward the door. She had to get out of here!

"Why? Do you think I don't have the guts?"

Val saw the gleam in his eyes and knew that she had to choose her words carefully. The slightest provocation would set him off.

"I think you're too decent."

Earl laughed, a hollow laugh that was devoid of mirth. "You're right; I am decent, but I'm also angry. The poets were right when they said 'hell hath no fury,' but it's not just women who are scorned."

Val lunged for the doorknob, no longer worrying about Earl's reaction. It was too late for that. All that mattered was getting out the door.

"You can't get out." He laughed again, and this time there was a note of frenzy in his laughter. "It's double-locked." He reached into his pocket and pulled out his key ring, dangling it on his index finger. "Come and get it," he invited.

The man was mad. "I'll scream," Val warned.

"Scream away." Earl turned up the volume on the stereo. "No one will hear you."

Her face turned ashen. How could she have been so mistaken as to think Earl needed her help? The man had obviously schemed and plotted for days, just to get her here.

"You won't force me," she said, her words little more than a plea.

Earl stared at her, his eyes glazed with an emotion Val could not identify. For a moment, she wasn't even sure he knew who was standing in front of him. Then he moved with startling swiftness.

She should have expected it, should have been prepared, but when he reached for her, Val was so frightened that she froze.

"Don't make me force you," Earl panted, gripping her upper arms. He pulled her closer, pinning her against his body with one arm while the other hand drew her face to his. His lips were so near, she could feel the warmth of his breath.

Oh, God! What am I going to do? Val cried to herself. She turned her face aside in disgust, and Earl's lips grazed her ear.

"Playing hard to get?" he asked. "That's fine with me. Victory will be all the sweeter after a struggle." He grasped her tighter, and the keys he still held in his hand cut into her arm.

The pain broke through the haze of fear

that had paralyzed Val. "You're hurting me, Earl," she cried.

But he did not appear to hear her. Once again he lowered his head, trying to capture her lips with his, and the keys dug further into Val's arm.

"You're hurting me," she sobbed, tears of pain stinging her eyes.

This time her plea got through to him. Startled, Earl dropped his arms, and the key ring clattered to the floor. He gazed at Val, her face contorted with pain. "I'm sorry," he said as though from a great distance. As Val rubbed her arm, trying to assuage the pain, Earl's expression softened. "I didn't mean to hurt you," he said.

Val didn't respond. He sounded sincere, but how could she tell? He had sounded sincere before. This might be some new trick.

He looked down at the floor. "I didn't mean it." Wearily he stooped to pick up the keys, then shuffled to the door like an old man, as though the effort of crossing the room were more than he could manage. He unlocked the door and turned. "Don't hate me," he cried, and crumpled to the floor.

Instantly Val hurried to his side and knelt next to him. "I don't hate you," she said, and strangely, it was true. This man had just threatened her and hurt her, but she did not hate him. How could she? He was a broken man, an object of pity rather than hatred. "I'm worried about you, Earl. I think you're in real trouble."

He was huddled on the floor with his head in his hands. "What should I do?" he asked, not looking at Val. "Go back to A.A., where they say they care and then stab you in the back?"

His cry was plaintive, and this time Val knew it was genuine. "Earl, A.A. didn't let you down."

He raised his eyes to hers. "No. Gary did."

Slowly Val nodded. "I know. He let us both down." Earl began to sob, and she put her arms around him. "You need help, Earl. You have to let someone help you."

And as the tears streamed down his face, Val comforted him as she would a child.

That was how Gary found them when he shoved open the door. "Are you all right?" he demanded as his eyes flew to Val, searching her face. If Earl had hurt her, he'd kill him!

Val nodded. "I'm fine."

In two quick strides, he reached them. Val's face bore the marks of tears and her smile was tremulous, but her eyes were clear. Gary expelled a sigh of relief. Val was okay!

"How does it feel to find your wife with another man?" Earl demanded harshly.

In response, Gary reached down and

took Val's hand, raising her to her feet. "I want you to keep away from my wife," he said, his voice calm but firm.

Earl stood up and faced Gary, his fists clenched. "What about what you did with my wife?"

Gary looked at him steadily for a moment. It was a question that had hung between them unanswered for too long. "Your wife did what she wanted to," he said finally. "Don't blame me for Judy's actions."

But Earl was not convinced. "I trusted you," he retorted.

Gary drew a hand through his blond hair in a gesture of despair. "I know. And I'm sorry." He put his arm around Val, silently telling her that the apology was directed to her, too. "I shouldn't have done it. I don't know if you believe me, but I'm sorry."

Val's face was shining with pride. She knew how difficult apologies were for Gary. Just saying the words "I'm sorry" was one of the hardest things he had ever done.

"Sorry's not good enough," Earl said, his face still reflecting his anger.

"It's all I can do," Gary said, and Val squeezed his arm. If Earl wouldn't accept the apology, that was his problem, not Gary's.

"You broke up my marriage."

Gary shook his head. He refused to accept the blame for that. "Earl, your marriage was falling apart before you ever met me."

Unable to deny Gary's statement, Earl tried again. "You were my friend . . ."

"I'm sorry I let you down, but you can't blame me for what's wrong with your life." Gary's eyes met Earl's in a silent duel. "Look to yourself, Earl. It's the only way you're going to salvage something out of this."

As Earl stared after them, Val and Gary left the apartment, their arms clasped around each other.

Laura was propped up on her pillow, leafing through a magazine when Richard climbed into bed.

"Laura . . . um . . ."

She tossed the magazine aside and looked at him, but he did not continue, just cleared his throat. Laura raised her eyebrows in surprise. This was not like Richard, usually so glib. Why was he suddenly hemming and hawing?

"Yes, Richard?" she prompted.

He looked at the wall, seemingly unable to meet her eyes. "We never talked much about what happened with me and Abby, did we?"

"No, we didn't." Laura was puzzled. Why was he bringing up Abby now? Was it because she had mentioned Abby earlier when they'd argued about her dinner with Scooter?

"Do you want to?"

Laura looked sharply at her husband. "Why? Do you plan to see her again?"

"No!" Richard swallowed and appeared to be considering his words carefully. "I just thought that maybe if we were more open about it, we might learn to trust each other more."

Trust! That was priceless, after the things he'd accused her of just this evening.

"What's the matter, Richard?" Her voice was sharp. "Don't you trust me?"

"Of course, I trust you. It's only that . . ." Richard moved restlessly.

"Only that what?" Laura had the feeling that this time she was the attorney, carefully drawing answers from the witness.

"You're very important to me," he said slowly, enunciating each word. "I don't want to lose you."

The words were so unexpected that for a moment Laura didn't know what to say. With all the recent tensions over Laura's professional success, Richard had begun to belittle her. She reached over and took Richard's hand, holding it to her cheek. "Thank you for saying that," she whispered.

He pulled her hand back and pressed a kiss into the palm.

"So, nothing happened, right?" he asked.

"Happened?"

Richard seemed embarrassed. "You know; you and Scooter."

Laura smiled, remembering her evening with Scooter. Something had happened, but not the something Richard was afraid of.

"Scooter and I are friends," she said.

"But there are friends, and there are *friends*."

"We're just friends, Richard." Laura turned and kissed him. "Just friends," she repeated.

"Oh, Val, I feel like such a hypocrite." The pain in Gary's voice wrenched her heart.

"You have no reason to," she said firmly, slipping her arms around him. They were sitting in the living room, both of them too keyed up to think about sleeping.

"I told him to look to himself," Gary continued. "I should be saying the same thing to myself. If I hadn't gotten involved with Judy, none of this would have happened. You wouldn't have been hurt."

Val's blue eyes were earnest as she forced Gary to look at her. "Nothing bad has happened. There's nothing to forgive."

"I wish I could believe that."

"Believe it, Gary." She tightened her arms around him and whispered, "I love you," as she raised her face for his kiss.

Chapter Twelve
Surprise!

The car moved slowly down the cul-de-sac, its driver looking carefully at each house he passed, searching for someone or something. It was only when he reached the end that he stopped.

She wasn't outside. She ought to be home by now, but when he had called, there had been no answer. Where was she?

Kenny Ward climbed out of the car and approached the front door of what had once been his house. He fingered the keys in his pocket. Should he wait for Ginger inside? No, that would upset her. Even though she hadn't changed the locks as she had threatened, Kenny didn't want to risk going inside. That was one thing that bothered Ginger.

And that state of affairs bothered him. He'd been turned into a visitor in his own house. Still, he reflected, at least he had gotten that far. A few months ago, Ginger would barely speak to him; now they were going to Lamaze classes together, and she had agreed that he could assist in their baby's birth. Kenny often caught himself staring at the calendar in his office, wishing it were Tuesday, wishing every day were Tuesday, so that he could be with Ginger at the Lamaze class.

It wasn't enough, but it was a start.

With a determined look on his face, Kenny walked back to his car.

"Val, can I bake the cake?" Diana's face was bright with excitement. "I saw the cutest cake shaped like a baby dress, and I want to make it."

Val glanced at Karen, silently asking her opinion. She knew that Karen wanted to include Diana in Ginger's shower as a recognition of her fledgling maturity, but Val had no idea whether or not Diana could cook.

Almost imperceptibly, Karen nodded.

"That would be terrific, Diana," Val said. "I'll have enough to do without worrying about making a cake."

Abby looked up from the table where she was sipping iced tea and wishing Gary would come home. She pointed at the wall next to Val's stove and gave a slightly malicious smile. "It's a good thing you have a fire extinguisher close at hand,

Val. I've found they're useful when *children* cook."

Her face red with embarrassment, Diana rushed from the room.

"Was that absolutely necessary, Abby?" Karen demanded. "Just because you couldn't bake a cake if your life depended on it doesn't mean that my daughter can't."

"Sorry." Abby mouthed the apology, but her tone lacked sincerity. She looked at her watch once more. "When do you think the men will be home?" she asked.

Karen smiled. Abby was about as subtle as a striking rattler. "Sid said something about inventory tonight. I imagine he and Gary will be late."

As Karen had expected, Abby soon found a reason to go home. "Good riddance," she said when Abby had left.

Val nodded absentmindedly as she finished the list of groceries to buy for Ginger's shower.

I wonder if Val even suspects what Abby is up to, Karen thought. *Probably not.*

"Want to stop for a sandwich on the way home?" Sid asked. The inventory had taken longer than he had anticipated, and it was past ten.

Gary nodded. His stomach had been growling for the past two hours. A sandwich—or two or three—was just what he needed. Since both men had their cars, they arranged to rendezvous at a nearby coffee shop.

"I wish we could catch those vandals," Gary said as he and Sid waited for their food.

"You worry more than I do," Sid said with a laugh. "Not that I'm complaining— it's great having someone share the worries." He paused while the waitress set the plates in front of them. "I'm not much of one for words. Karen always complains that I forget to tell people the important things, and she's probably right. But I do want to say that I'm glad you joined Knots Landing Motors. Hiring you was one of the smartest moves I've ever made."

Gary mumbled a reply and lowered his eyes, suddenly afraid to meet Sid's gaze. If only Sid knew . . .

Sid's words echoed in Gary's mind as he drove home: "One of the smartest moves I've ever made." Would he say that if he knew about the Orchid Cab Company? About Gary's secret dealings with thugs like Roy Lance? Not likely.

When he was almost at the cul-de-sac, an odd prickling started on the back of his neck. It was nothing he could define, just a sense that something was wrong. After hesitating for a moment, he turned the car around and headed back to the dealership.

It was purely instinct that made him

turn off the lights and park on the other side of the street. Purely instinct that made him seek the shadows and walk carefully. Instinct served him well, for when he reached the dealership, he could hear the sound of breaking glass and the cries of triumph as another brick hit its mark.

Damn them! Gary thought. He clenched his fists and lunged forward. He'd catch those vandals, nab them red-handed. And when he got them— But then common sense intervened. From the sounds of their voices, there were at least half a dozen of them. What chance did he have against that many?

Gary retreated, walked quickly to the phone booth on the corner and called the police. Within minutes the vandals' cries had changed from victory to defeat, and Gary was smiling.

His debt to Sid was not canceled, but at least he had made the first payment. Only one question remained: Were these vandals just rowdy teenagers, or were they professional thugs, hired by Gary's new "partners"?

"Do you think Ginger suspects?" Diana asked as she helped Val set the table.

"I don't think so. I told her I wanted company because Gary is going to be out tonight. There's no reason for her to think it's a shower."

"Besides, it's a little early. Most of the showers for her won't be for another month," Karen added as she put Diana's cake on the sideboard. Despite Abby's malicious comment, the cake had turned out perfectly.

The dining room was festooned with balloons and a large parasol was suspended from the ceiling, while gaily wrapped packages covered one table. Several women were chattering in the living room. Everything was almost ready.

"Ready?" the woman asked.

The car crept down the street, its lights extinguished even though darkness had fallen. The driver, peering intently through the slits of his ski mask, relied on house lights to guide him. They were almost there.

"This damned mask is too tight," the other man complained. His voice was muffled by the wool mask, but it was still loud enough to make the woman cringe.

"Sssh!" she hissed. "They'll hear you."

"How the hell are they gonna hear me when the windows are rolled up?"

"Quiet!" the driver commanded. "We ain't takin' no chances."

"There you are," Karen said as Laura and Abby came in through the back door. "I was afraid Ginger would beat you."

"Oh, Scooter had to go over some

listings with me," Laura explained.

"And I forgot the flowers until I got all the way home. I had to go back into town to the florist."

Val sniffed Abby's floral arrangement before she put them in the center of the table. "They're gorgeous!" she said. "Thanks for bringing them."

"Anything, just so I don't have to cook." Abby laughed and straightened her hair as she glanced in the mirror.

Everything was ready. All they needed was the guest of honor.

"Isn't it time?" the man in the backseat demanded. "I can't stand this waiting."

"Soon," the driver promised. "Wait till that woman gets inside." In the darkness he could barely see the figure waiting on the front doorstep. "You got everything ready?" He turned and looked at the man behind him. "You got the pieces?"

"You bet." There was a chuckle of anticipation.

"You don't think she's forgotten, do you?" Diana worried.

"I'm sure she hasn't," Laura reassured her. "Ginger'll be here any minute now."

As though on cue, the doorbell chimed and Ginger walked in.

"Surprise!" Diana cried. The other women joined the chorus. "Surprise, Ginger!"

* * *

"Now!"

It was the moment they had waited for, the moment they had dreamed about. Softly, the car door opened and a man climbed out. He glanced around nervously, then darted toward the large bush in front of the house. Carefully, not making a sound, he slipped behind it. The spot was perfect. Standing to one side, he could peer indoors. It was just as they had thought, just as they had planned.

With a smile of anticipation, he signaled to his cohorts. The adventure was about to begin.